Miriam

Repentance and Redemption in Rome

Cheryl Dickow

© 2013 by Cheryl Dickow

Published by Bezalel Books, Waterford, MI

www.BezalelBooks.com

The choicest first fruits of your soil you shall bring to the

house of the Lord, your God.

~Exodus 23.79

Printed in the United States of America

Edith Stein quote is used with permission. It is taken from *The Hidden Life* Translated by Waltraut Stein, Ph.D. Copyright (c) 1992 by Washington Province of Discalced Carmelites ICS Publication 2131 Lincoln Road, N.E. Washington, DC 20002-1199 U.S.A. www.icspublications.org

Cover art Starblue | Dreamstime.com

ISBN 978-1-936453-14-6

Library of Congress Control Number 2013903950

Dear Reader,

This is a work of fiction, although I have enjoyed weaving truths within its pages. After all, you probably know that Edith Stein and Padre Pio were real; but maybe you've never heard of St. Sharbel—and if that is the case I hope that reading a bit about him will bless you. Prayers such as the *Amidah* and the *Pardon Prayer* are real. Some facts about geographical locations written about in this work of fiction are true, too. You get the idea.

Miriam is somewhat of a sequel to my first work of fiction *Elizabeth: A Holy Land Pilgrimage*—although one needn't have read *Elizabeth* to read *Miriam* (but I certainly hope that if you didn't, this will entice you to do so!). It is a long time in the making. Maybe because God had to use a number of people to nudge me along and show me that it was time to write this book. These people include friends like Pam, Valerie, Nancy, Gerri, Chris, Amy, and Annette and also some interesting "signs" from the Almighty Himself; but nothing would be possible if it weren't for my husband John who has far greater confidence in me than I could ever have in myself. I also need to thank Andrea for her immense help in gathering information about the works of Edith Stein.

Ultimately, my prayer is that every reader of *Miriam: Repentance and Redemption in Rome* is blessed by the work. I certainly was in listening to God and writing it for you!

The Scripture quotes I used within this work are taken from either *The Navarre Bible* or *Saint Joseph Edition of the New American Bible* (I love both!). Other quotes I used came from the following works that I have read over the years and have cherished: *The Big Book of Christian Mysticism* by Carl McColman; *Andersen's Fairy Tales* by Hans Christian Andersen; *Summa Theologica* by St. Thomas Aquinas; *The Divine Comedy* by Dante; *Edith Stein: An Autobiography*; *The Glory Within* by Corey Russell; *The Journey* by Billy Graham; *The Privilege of Being a Woman* by Alice von Hildebrand.

Cheryl Dickow

God is love.

Miriam's earliest memories were of this truth. Her parents, Meir and Ayala, imparted that reality to her and her brother, David, in a variety of ways. Some of the ways in which Miriam absorbed this truth were quite subtle. Others were not. Attending Akiva Day School would have fallen into the latter category although as Miriam grew up she understood that it was a necessary part of becoming a faithful Jew—even if, as a youngster, she saw the required studying as infringing upon her time. Nonetheless, she also realized that the gentle, restrained ways in which her parents taught her about God's love were just as valuable. They were committed to each other and to their children. They served God by serving others. Their hearts and home were always open. As she reflected upon it all now, she saw that the book learning that took place at school seeped deep into her head while the experiences of life in the Goldfarb home seeped depth within her heart.

Together, they wove the tapestry of Miriam's faith life and although the death of her mother in a bombing seemed to rip through the very fabric, it did not, in the end, destroy it. Miriam's love for God, her understanding of his love for her, and the journey to her destiny hinged on that one undeniable truth: God is love.

Chapter One

Peace in society depends upon peace in the family.

~ St. Augustine

There were good days and there were bad days. If Miriam tallied them, she would see that the good days outweighed the bad—even while the dark ones often seemed unbearable.

When those emotionally draining days hit, it felt as if Ayala's death was something that would forever haunt Miriam, forever hold her. On particularly difficult days, Miriam avoided looking in the mirror; she did not want to see the shadowy hand upon her shoulder, unwilling to let her go. It was enough that Miriam felt as if she was in a constant battle to escape the clammy hold it had on her as it clamored for her attention—she did not need to see it as well, convinced as she was in those moments of its real and physical presence in her life. She abhorred how it seized opportunities to take up residence in her mind. It seemed as if the slightest thing had the capacity to galvanize Miriam's mind on the tragedy: the sights, sounds, and smells of that day would envelop her as she would perceive yet again the human carnage and suffering; her ears would hear the sounds of screaming and moaning and crying; she could actually smell burnt flesh and the acrid smoke that filled the air.

But for every difficult day, God had granted Miriam times of renewal. He did not abandon her, nor did He forsake her. His grace and mercy were endless. Like the Sabbath candles that were lit each Friday to usher in God's presence, God would not let the light of his love be overwhelmed by the darkness that attempted to swallow up Miriam. And although it took some time, Miriam found that walking through the marketplace had become, once again, a time of pleasure and joy. She could stand at a stall and hear her mother's voice exchanging pleasantries with the merchant, inquiring as to prices and freshness. During those times Miriam's heart was flooded with love. She grinned from ear to ear and knew that passersby assumed that her grin was due to a particularly good deal she must have struck with a merchant; but it was so much more benign than that. During those times where Miriam walked through the marketplace, peace radiating from the depths of her heart, it was because Adonai had pulled back the curtain between heaven and earth; He had given Miriam a glimpse of the eternal love that was hers regardless of pain that, from time to time, existed within her heart. Hashem, blessed be His holy name, was holding Miriam in the palm of His hand.

Ayala died before she had learned of Miriam's love for Joseph. Joseph was a kind and gentle man. Miriam met him during her brief time in Mossad—Israel's Institute for Intelligence and Special Operations. Prior to the bombing, Miriam fully expected to remain a Mossad agent; but, her mother's death forced her to evaluate that choice. Ayala had known of Miriam's decision to join the elite group and had fervently prayed that it would not become Miriam's final destination.

"Emma, I want to help make this world a better place. I want to defend our country against all that is coming against it. I want..."

Miriam couldn't finish her sentence because she could see the pain in her mother's eyes. Rightfully so, Ayala knew the risks that would forever be part of her daughter's life if she remained an agent. She just could not bring herself to condone—let alone bless—this sort of decision. Quietly Ayala asked her daughter a question that would haunt Miriam afterwards and force her hand, "But is this what God wants of you?"

To that point, Miriam had not really considered what God wanted of her life.

Chapter Two

*It had been revealed to him by the Holy
Spirit that he should not see death before
he had seen the Messiah of the Lord.*

~ Luke 2:26

During Miriam's time at Mossad, Meir learned to rely on Adonai in new and deeper ways. He also had to learn how to shut down his vivid imagination or he would drive himself crazy with fear and worry about his daughter. While both Meir and Ayala had always been observant Jews, when Miriam joined Mossad, Meir never let go of God's ear. He spoke to the Blessed Creator morning, noon, and night.

Meir also prayed for the other members of Mossad. There were agents bringing Jews safely home from different countries or pursuing war criminals. Success stories included the infamous Adolf Eichmann, brought to trial in Israel for war crimes. But Meir knew that unsuccessful stories were probably far more common, even though their details went unknown.

Mossad was also involved in the strategic planning and implementation of elite missions outside of Israel's borders. They were the main players when it came to preventing hostile nations from developing nuclear and biological weapons. The United States depended on these covert operations to maintain safety within their own borders. Although a fateful day in September certainly proved to the great American nation that terror and terrorism was a worldwide epidemic. No one, no country, was excluded.

Of all the agents that Meir prayed for, Joseph quickly rose to the top of his list. This was because of Miriam's love for him. Both David and Meir had only briefly met Joseph but it became very clear why Miriam was smitten. Indeed it was probably more obvious to everyone except the two who were clearly in love! Prior to meeting Joseph, Miriam had shared with both Meir and David different stories that always revolved around him; both Meir and David needed only to listen to Miriam to know there was so much more to her relationship with Joseph than just the work they did together. They seemed connected in a very real, very deep way.

"Abba," began one of Miriam's calls.

"Yes?" Meir had hastily responded. He could already tell by the tone of Miriam's voice that something was following that would take him by surprise.

"Abba, I was hoping we could get together this weekend and celebrate Sabbath."

It was an odd request because the children spent almost every Sabbath, when possible, at home. *Why wouldn't they celebrate as they always did?* "Of course, isn't that what we always do?" was Meir's questioning answer.

"Well, yes, but this will be a little different. I would like to bring someone home for you to meet. And David, I would like David to meet him, too." Miriam quickly added, "You may remember, I've talked about him before. His name is Youssef, although he goes by the more common version Joseph. He is also with Mossad, an agent, like me. And his family is away on vacation."

"Of course I remember you speaking of him! I would love to meet him. You know that any friend of yours is always welcome at our Sabbath celebration. It is a mitzvah to do such a thing and I will joyfully set another place for this Youssef—Joseph—your friend."

Miriam responded with a simple, but heartfelt, thank you, "Toda!"

Yes, the more Meir knew about Mossad, the less he wished he knew. The degree to which his government had to go to keep abreast of the activities of the changing and challenging world no longer fascinated him. Now he was just horrified at the extent to which nations would go in attempt to annihilate one another. At the moment, all eyes were on the United States as one of the most important pieces of legislation ever to be introduced was going to be voted upon. It was an abortion tax that gave sweeping power—and funding—to support abortion throughout their country. Most legal experts from countries far and wide anticipated its successful passage into law but only two rabbis from Israel were willing to speak out against what they were calling the atrocity of the 21st century. Meir suspected that more people agreed with these two rabbis than were willing to admit. And whether you agreed or disagreed, everyone understood that this law would not only sweep across the United States but like a strong trade wind would sweep across the globe. It was already causing riots in the streets of America and reverberations everywhere else. Citizens from nations far and wide were holding their breath.

All of it made Meir truly wonder if peace were only a fable, told to children to build up their dreams about the world that they were inheriting. But they were dreams that Miriam had come to believe in; Meir understood that this was why she became a Mossad agent: that nations could and should live in peace.

And that Sabbath dinner now seemed like a lifetime ago.

Chapter Three

*Do not neglect to show hospitality to
strangers, for thereby some have
entertained angels unawares.*

~ Hebrews 13:2

"Shalom! You must be Joseph. Welcome to our home."
Miriam knew she could count on her father to warmly
receive Joseph. She was proud at how kind and
compassionate her parents were to everyone they met.
Miriam fondly recalled how they had taken in Elizabeth,
an American woman who had vacationed in Israel only
a handful of years ago.

On occasion, Miriam would find a note from
Elizabeth on the kitchen counter. They had all kept in
touch to one degree or another. Each of their lives had
been changed in those few weeks, maybe Elizabeth's the
most—so it made sense that they all stayed connected.
She was part of their extended family now. Even though
land and water physically separated them they were
bound together in a very spiritual sense.

Elizabeth had been with their family, spending a day
at the marketplace, when the bomb exploded and killed
Ayala. So whenever Elizabeth dropped a note to Meir,
Miriam was reminded that God truly can bring good
from bad. Elizabeth could have fled to her homeland—
to her life in America—and made the decision to never
again look back at the tragedy that was part of her trip;
but, instead, she saw love among the people who
survived the bombing: Israeli's tending to the wounds
of Palestinians and Muslims helping Christians. In those
few moments after the attack, everyone was the same in

their grief and in their sorrow. The love that must surely exist in the center of each and every heart became apparent and Elizabeth seemed to keep that with her instead of the death that day. Elizabeth could have taken the path of least resistance and never looked back at her trip to the Holy Land; but she didn't. She had shown herself to be a remarkable woman and friend to the Goldfarbs.

Miriam would be the first to say that her government and the Israeli people weren't always on the receiving end of these acts. No, Miriam found that there were no longer clear lines between right and wrong, good and bad, black and white.

Lost in her thoughts, Miriam had missed whatever her father had said to Joseph and was now only hearing his response.

"Shalom! Yes, I am Joseph and it is so kind of you to open your home to me this Sabbath evening."

"We are always honored when Adonai, blessed be His Holy Name, allows us to perform a mitzvah. So, please, say nothing more about it."

Joseph walked into the Goldfarb apartment and waited for his host to gesture for him to sit. Meir liked that courtesy and noticed that Joseph was shoulder to shoulder in height to his Miriam. She was tall like her brother. Meir imagined how Ayala would be thinking that Joseph and Miriam were a beautiful couple, even if they weren't a couple. Miriam with dark, thick hair and beautiful almond shaped eyes with a thin but beautiful figure. Meir fondly recalled how Ayala, in her own youth, very much resembled Miriam at this age. Both their children received their height from Ayala. Joseph had a head of thick reddish-brown hair with a slight curl. It was short, as required by Mossad, but it clearly had a wave to it. His eyes were also brown and his nose less Mediterranean than Miriam's.

Just then David walked out of the bedroom and welcomed Joseph, "Shalom! How are you? I am David Goldfarb, Miriam's brother."

Joseph extended his hand to take David's and smiled.

David said, "Please, sit down." Then in the next breath added, "Abba, dinner smells wonderful!"

Meir had always helped Ayala in the kitchen and in particular enjoyed preparing the Sabbath meal at her side. Doing all the cooking on his own now had become his saving grace. He spent the time deep in prayer and in thoughts about his beloved wife. His heart was filled during those times with a torrent of emotions. *How could he have been so blessed by Yahweh to have had such a dear and kind wife? Would his own children find the happiness that both he and Ayala had experienced? Would he ever become a grandfather and would that bring pain or joy to his heart? Pain from not sharing the experience with Ayala—or joy at new blessings?*

Forcing himself even now from his revelry, Meir chuckled and then responded to David's compliment about dinner, "David, you say that every Sabbath! You will surely be a blessing to your congregation." David had accepted a rabbinic position at a local synagogue.

Meir then faced Joseph and asked where his parents were. It was clear that he wasn't nosey as much as simply curious. Joseph's parents must have had the same characteristics because he did not get uncomfortable at the inquiry. "Twice a year my parents travel to the United States to visit my mother's family. She is from Massachusetts."

"Have you traveled there as well?" Meir wanted to know.

"Yes, many times while I was growing up. I have two older sisters and our parents loved to take us to the states. And I have to say, we loved it, too! My sisters and I would pretend that we lived in the big homes and had many cars and went to the best schools. Now that I look back, I have to laugh at myself. But, we had so much fun."

"And where are your sisters? Do they live in Israel?" David joined the conversation.

"Yes, they do. My oldest sister, Sarah, is married and has four children. She lives not far from here. Her husband is a professor at the university. And you know my other sister, Sipporah. Sipporah was actually named after my father's grandmother. Anyhow, she and Miriam have been friends for many years now."

David said, "Please, let's make our way to the dinner table before the sun sets and we have missed our call to light the Sabbath candles. We can continue our conversation after we have asked God to bless our meal and our gathering."

Everyone stood, in agreement, and walked over to the beautifully set table as Miriam remarked, "Abba, I always think of Emma in a special way at our Sabbath meals. I wonder if I will ever be able to present a Sabbath meal to my own family that is as wonderful as ours have been here."

Miriam's love and respect for her parents seemed to have increased with age. Both children were basically good kids when they were young but they still brought their fair share of grief into the lives of their parents. Lately, however, Meir was seeing the fruits of his and

Ayala's parenting labor. Their children were kind and compassionate and respectful. They spoke with an honesty and integrity that brought peace to Meir's spirit. At that moment, he desired nothing more than to assuage his daughter's heart, "Miriam! You will be a most magnificent wife and mother and will honor God with wonderful Sabbath dinners for your family. You will be a balabusta to be sure!"

David caught Joseph's reaction to this statement about Miriam being a "balabusta"—a good homemaker, a fine wife and mother—and smiled quietly to himself. It was obvious that there was more here than Miriam was sharing—or maybe more than she herself knew.

Everyone stood behind their chairs and Miriam lit the Sabbath candles and recited the blessing:

Barukh atah Adonai, Eloheinu, melekh ha'olam asher kidishanu b'mitz'votav v'tzivanu l'had'lik neir shel Shabbat. Amein.

When she was done with her prayers, she moved the lit candles to a sideboard and they all took their seats.

Meir stood before a rather large soup tureen and ladled steaming hot matzoh ball soup into bowls that were passed until each person had one. As if on cue, everyone began talking at once and Meir heartily called out, "My! I can see we have a lot of catching up to do but if I remember correctly—and I don't always remember correctly anymore—Joseph was going to share his genealogy with us."

"Oh dear me! I do apologize Joseph! I completely forgot that I scuttled us off to the table right as you were about to begin." It was clear that David was sincerely sorry for having forgotten that he had interrupted Joseph just a few short minutes ago.

"Please, do not apologize, David…I don't want to bend anyone's ear nor bore them with the details of my life."

"Believe me, Joseph; we are no doubt more curious about you than we are probably willing to admit!" David always had a way of pointing out the obvious but in a kind and loving way. Meir beamed with a father's pride just thinking about David as a rabbi and how lovingly, but fairly, he would minister to his duties.

Chapter Four

*Let brotherly love continue. Do not neglect
hospitality, for through it some have
unknowingly entertained angels.*

~ Hebrews 13:1-2

"Let's see," Joseph began. "My mother is from Massachusetts. She was in college when she met my father. Both were at Williams College but my mother was a sophomore and my father a senior. Dad has a Jewish background and mom is Christian. They met in an international business course which my father was enrolled in for his degree in business and my mother was taking, I guess, on a whim. She had always imagined travelling the globe and she was really just beginning to consider what her major would be. At any rate, the two clashed!"

With that, all eyes that had been going back and forth between finishing up the delicious soup and listening to Joseph were squarely focused on Joseph. David chuckled in his good-natured way and said, "I'm so glad this isn't a 'they fell in love at first sight and lived happily ever after' story! Go on, man, let's hear more!"

The blush that rose in Miriam's cheeks at the mention of "love at first sight" didn't escape Meir whose interest in Joseph immediately increased ten-fold.

"Well, the way they tell it—and they are both pretty much on the same page with their versions of their meeting—is that the professor was putting forth some idea about the global economy, how we are all becoming interdependent on one another and also obligated to one another when my father heard my mother 'snort' her disagreement with the professor. Apparently it went unnoticed by the lecturer but my dad was intrigued and approached my mother after class."

Joseph enjoyed a few spoonfuls of his soup, before it became too cold, and David offered, "Forgive us, Joseph, you are not our dinner entertainment! Please, enjoy your soup and allow me to begin passing our meal."

"This is absolutely delicious!" was all Joseph said in the way of an agreement as he finished his soup and handed the empty bowl to Miriam who then collected them all from the table and walked them to the kitchen.

As Miriam returned and then served the meal of roasted chicken and wonderful mixed greens, Joseph continued. "My father approached my mother in the hall after class and asked if she would mind explaining her 'snort' in regards to the idea of a global economy and social obligations on an international level. My mother, though passionate about social justice and issues of poverty and education and caring for one another, has very clear feelings about being in a situation where those sorts of responses are anything other than personal ones. In other words, as she told my father that day, she didn't feel that citizens of any country could be coerced to 'care' about others. My mother felt—feels—that these are the values that we learn at home and should not be government regulated or initiated."

"I can see her point," Meir offered. "After all, as Jews we believe that there are things we are asked to do to become Adonai's hands, in a way, but when we do them because we are forced to then they lose their value to us. They lose their merit. As Jews we believe that our Creator, Blessed be He, loves us so much that He gives us constant ways to serve Him by serving others; but that service only has reward when we do it because of our love of Him."

"Well, Meir, it looks like you and my mother share a common philosophy. My dad, on the other hand, could not have disagreed more. From his perspective, and I admit understanding it all too well, people don't always help others in ways that they are able to—or should. What my father believes is that there is a goodness that can be gained for a person who otherwise wouldn't have had that goodness had it been solely up to his own decision-making process."

"Good point," David interjected. "Sometimes we lose sight of the fact that these two religions have, at their core, the basic belief in human dignity and from that dignity we are called to care for others less fortunate. 'Judeo-Christian' is what I believe many Americans call this faith history. Anyhow, while we all agree on some things, we often disagree on how things might be accomplished."

Smiling, Joseph added, "Well, for my parents that 'heated' exchange did lead to 'sparks.' What began as an attempt to convince one another that they each were right, ended with both seeing a different side to that issue—and countless more in the years to come. In many ways I admire the leap of faith they took into each other's arms because their religious differences were no small obstacle in their path."

"So," Meir asked while wiping his mouth with his napkin, "how did they ever reconcile their religious differences when they had you children?"

"As you might imagine, neither extended family whole-heartedly welcomed the inter-faith marriage. To put some distance between themselves and their families and allow their marriage to take root, my parents actually moved to France for the first couple of years after my father's graduation. My mother finished up her education in the 'City of Lights' while my father pursued a degree in international finance. My sister, Sarah, was born in France.

"Somehow, somewhere along the way, my mother—who remember had always wanted to travel the world—realized that she had to make a full commitment to my father and his life; this meant moving to Israel, to my father's home. It also required her to delve more deeply into the roots of her Christian faith where she found a common bond that has held them together all these years. Those decisions—to move to Israel and understand her faith more deeply—seemed to create a moment of truth for my mother's family. My maternal grandparents were not willing to lose their daughter in both a spiritual as well as a physical sense. They did what they could to mend fences and welcome my father into their lives.

"Before their final move to Israel, my parents returned to Massachusetts with Sarah—at that point a toddler—where my grandparents spent time learning to love their son-in-law and building a foundation with their granddaughter that continues to this day."

Miriam sat with her hands in her lap, never tired of hearing about the love that Joseph's parents have for each other and knowing that Joseph had inherited that great capacity of love, self-sacrifice, and wisdom.

Chapter Five

*The choicest first fruits of your soil you
shall bring to the house of the Lord your
God.*

~ Exodus 23:19

David suggested making a pot of coffee and taking it out onto the small balcony off the Goldfarb apartment. A few stories up, the Goldfarbs always enjoyed the early evening breeze that gently brought traffic sounds wafting to their residence. Sabbath evenings were especially quiet, though, as most people did not use their cars, and that quiet brought a peace all its own. The Goldfarbs were not orthodox Jews who would not use electrical appliances on the Sabbath; so while they honored the Sabbath by attending Synagogue and reciting all the traditional blessings over the bread and wine—and Miriam always lit the Sabbath candles—they would still take advantage of the conveniences of such things as their coffee maker. On occasion David had shared his personal struggle as he often felt torn between practicing his faith in the truest, most Orthodox way, and being a more liberal, even "modern," Jew.

Both Meir and Ayala appreciated that their son was so open with them and knew that if David's misgivings about practicing the faith in a non-Orthodox way became too burdensome, he would change and they would uphold and respect that decision. They had always kept a kosher home and knew that this was very much appreciated by David. To this day, Meir abided by these things that he and Ayala had put into place. It was

Meir's way of respecting his son and honoring his wife's memory.

While coffee was being made—a thick, aromatic blend of beans that made Joseph immediately think of his father's own favorite coffee—David and Meir set up a couple of extra chairs on the balcony and pulled out a tray table from the closet that would serve the two additional chairs. The stars glistened in the sky and the few clouds drifted along minding their own business—with nary a care in the world, oblivious to the planet below. It was a truly beautiful evening.

Meanwhile, Miriam cleared the dinner table and readied the compote dessert bowls. Ayala had perfected a number of different dessert recipes over the years but the family had most thoroughly enjoyed fruit compote. Served warm or cold, compote used the freshest fruits from the market with their juices melding together in a magical way. When the kids were young, and had experienced the hurt or pain of a particularly difficult adolescent day, Ayala always found that compote drew them out of their misery and filled their stomachs with the sort of love that also nourished their souls; then, in the morning, everything appeared tolerable. A new day could begin.

Joseph was now enjoying the bustle in the apartment and could see that this was a routine that had been perfected over time. Family, Joseph knew, really was the cornerstone of society. Somehow his parents had managed to bless their children—Sarah, Sipporah and Joseph—with this understanding of family and faith in God Almighty.

Feeling a quickening in his chest, Joseph also knew the time was fast approaching when he would have to tell Miriam that he was being asked to take a future assignment in Lebanon that had very real, very dangerous implications. It didn't go unnoticed to Joseph that more and more of the assignments seemed to be crossing over into what he would have called the "spiritual" or "religious" arena. Assignments that were once strictly political were now quasi-political-religious. Mossad was even recruiting non-Israeli personnel in a new arm of the organization that was working with the global aspects of national security that crossed these geopolitical-religious lines. Joseph only had to consider the immediate Four Horsemen mission to confirm this; it was one part religion, one part politics. That was what the assignment in Lebanon was also going to be: one part religion, one part politics. Apparently there was a tomb of a saint that was being overrun with political factions. It was well known that governments wanting to create a despairing and despondent populace do so by removing the hope and peace that is derived from faith. Thus the tomb was in jeopardy of being destroyed since it represented to believers the truth of Christ through a simple, obedient man's life and death.

Religious zeal worried—even frightened—governments eager to control their citizens. And with Lebanon so close to Israel, it was determined that Mossad would have to have a presence. The saint's name was Sharbel Markluf. He was also called the "Hermit of Lebanon" and it was clear that thousands of people believed in the miracles performed at his hands and after his death—thus the Catholic Church's beatification of Sharbel on December 5, 1965.

Joseph had to admit that he found the entire process of beatification incredibly interesting and did his own research into Sharbel when first hearing of his upcoming assignment.

†

Sharbel wasn't one of those irrelevant saints from eons ago—as so many were in Joseph's eyes. At one point, Joseph felt that some of the people he knew worshipped saints but then his mother set the record straight. She explained to him that the communion of saints were simply those people who had already entered into their eternal life and were still "friends" with those still on their earthly journey. Everything she said made sense—she was clever to appeal to Joseph's logic. By the time she was done, Joseph couldn't say he was converted to her way of thinking but he certainly saw it with more understanding.

She really laid the foundation for Joseph to be able to thoroughly research Sharbel who was born May 8, 1828 in a village in the mountains of Northern Lebanon. Sharbel was part of the Eastern Church. Knowing his own family history on his father's side, Joseph was able to relate to Sharbel's life: like so many of the families in his country, his was poor. Sharbel was the last of five children born to devout parents. He was baptized with the name Joseph. That seemed a very interesting coincidence.

As Joseph gathered this information about Sharbel he found himself having a renewed interest in his own mother's faith and upbringing; he was very grateful for the handful of conversations they had engaged in as she lovingly and patiently answered his sincere questions. From what Joseph read, Sharbel's parents raised their children with an eye toward eternity. This meant a detachment from things of the world and a constant development of an interior, spiritual life. Joseph was actually surprised that Sharbel was twenty-three when he left home to become a novice at a monastery. Joseph would have bet that raised in such a family Sharbel would have been much younger.

Nevertheless, Joseph wasn't surprised to read that Sharbel made vows of poverty, chastity, and obedience at which point he went from being known as Joseph to being called Sharbel—the name of an oriental martyr. Sharbel, however, went much further than Joseph could ever imagine: he completely abandoned his previous life; he wouldn't even see his mother. Although since Sharbel's maternal uncles were already living their lives as solitary monks at the Hermitage of Saint Paul in the Qadisha Valley, Joseph imagined Sharbel's mother, in some sense, may have even known this was going to be the life her youngest child pursued. *Maybe she was even a bit prophetic,* Joseph thought.

Faced with this knowledge, Joseph grappled with the idea of completely cutting yourself off from home and family and couldn't quite imagine how this could be pleasing to God; yet Joseph recognized within the marriage of his parents how people can and will do things they believe in even if it seems quite unnatural to the outside world. For that, Joseph had to commend Sharbel and murmured to no one in particular, "May God bless you for your faithfulness."

Two men were very influential in the development of Sharbel's monastic life: Reverend Father Nimitallah Al-Kafri and the Reverend Father Nimitallah Kassab Al-Hardini. Joseph thought of the people who were instrumental in his own journey and Miriam immediately came to mind. When Joseph was with her he felt completely covered in love and kindness—it was Miriam's way, no doubt the result of her upbringing. She was gifted with a giving and compassionate heart. Anyone with whom she interacted was surely given a permanent place in Miriam's prayer life.

Joseph solemnly wondered if he made a difference in anyone's life.

As he continued to read how Al-Kafri and Al-Hardini affected Sharbel and solidified his commitment to a virtuous life, Joseph quickly reviewed his own personal and professional relationships. *Had God asked him to be a beacon of light or hope or inspiration to anyone? And if He had, did Joseph succeed or fail?* Reading through all his papers on Sharbel made Joseph promise himself—and God—to more consciously interact with all people. Again, speaking to no one in particular, Joseph verbally avowed, "God, Heavenly Father, right here, right now, I pledge my life to you. In the freedom of this moment I give you everything that I have, everything that I will ever possess is not mine but is Yours. I'm not even sure what that will look like, but from the depths of my heart I want to follow St. Sharbel's lead: I want to live my life for You. I promise to open my heart to Your will and Your ways. I commit myself to seeing You in all things and being open to Your guidance and Your hand upon my life. I will do what You ask me to do. I will see what You invite me to see."

Once he finished, Joseph felt a bit silly and yet thought, *You just never know...*

He then chided himself for his lapse into the religious and continued studying Sharbel; but Joseph would soon see that his words, once spoken, would change his entire world.

"Okay, before you completely lose it, let's see what else you can learn about Sharbel to better prepare you for your work in Lebanon," Joseph said to himself as he opened a new book on the hermit of Lebanon. In the back of his mind Joseph also thought of the Four Horsemen mission that was immediately at hand and again marveled at how the political and religious aspects of his missions continued to overlap. *A sign of the times?* he wondered, even while knowing the answer. He knew that Abdul—a fellow agent recruited into the unusual multi-national arm of Mossad—would receive a special invitation to this mission after the Four Horsemen undertaking was complete. This was due to the fact that Lebanon was Abdul's homeland and he was especially familiar with the villages in the mountains.

Joseph's research continued. The more he learned about Sharbel, the more connected he felt to the saint and found himself asking for intercession—just like his mother explained was available to him through the communion of saints. "St. Sharbel, you followed God's will and joyfully accepted vows of poverty and chastity. You lived a monastic life and served all who God brought to you. As I undertake to do the same, please intercede for me as you more surely are aware of God's will as you enjoy His presence in Heaven. As you reside now in your eternal place, please accept my plea for your friendship and for your aid as I willingly offer myself to God."

There, couldn't hurt! was Joseph's more logical afterthought. He squirmed in his seat. *What is happening to me?* he seriously wondered before proceeding on.

Sharbel was ordained in July of 1859. He seemed to be an incredibly humble man and was responsible for performing Masses while also being responsible for the drudgery of a lot of manual labor around the monastery. Everything he did was done with humility, obedience, charity of spirit, and in total poverty and chastity. Joseph bristled at the idea of chastity. His mother had once told him that everyone is given different gifts— actually what she called charisms—and so while one person may be able to live a life of chastity, another will not. This didn't mean that it was a piece of cake for those who had the gift but that they would receive—as his mother said—special graces from God to live out those charisms. Made sense to Joseph and he smiled in appreciation that God did not give him that particular gift!

Sharbel spent almost two decades living this harsh existence before he was allowed to retire in 1875. This he did at the hermitage of Saints Peter and Paul in Annaya, which was two kilometers away from the Monastery of Saint Maroun. *No golfing for this guy!* Joseph chuckled to himself. Sharbel's retirement was made up of continued prayer, fasting, working, and being at the beck-and-call of his superiors. *Clearly these guys did not understand the concept of retirement,* Joseph thought as he continued reading. Joseph could see why one of the Catholic popes—Paul VI—said that Sharbel was a member of monastic sanctity. Joseph also realized that, as his mother had explained, no one could really do this without God's grace—and even then it was never easy! Thinking of all the people the world held up as heroes, Joseph realized that Sharbel was the true hero. Here was a man who spent his life in prayer and fasting and obedience to God. How many people could say the same thing about their own lives? Certainly very few—if any—of today's so-called "heroes."

Joseph wasn't exactly sure how the whole sainthood thing happened in the Catholic church but knew enough that before someone would be called—or declared—a saint there had to be miracles attributed to that person. For Sharbel those miracles began while he was still alive and included setting someone free from a snake (apparently Sharbel just needed to ask the snake to go away!) and curing a madman by simply saying a prayer. He also used holy water to free a field from a grasshopper invasion. It really all did sound juvenile to Joseph and yet he knew that this man's burial site was still being visited today by many pilgrims seeking his intercession—and that the site was also becoming a hotbed of political activity.

Sharbel died in 1898 after this austere and demanding life. And this is where it really got interesting. It was while he was celebrating Mass, during that critical time of transubstantiation, when he suffered a stroke while saying a prayer from part of the Maronite Liturgy. The prayer he said was, "Father of Truth, here is Your Son, Victim of Expiation; here is the Blood which intercedes for me, it is my offering, accept it." He never recovered from the stroke and existed in that plane between life and death for eight days.

All in all, his life consisted of sixteen years in a monastery followed by twenty-three in a hermitage. Every moment of every day lived in a remarkably holy way. Apparently he had a real devotion to the Eucharist and to the mother of Jesus. If it wasn't enough that he celebrated Mass every day, he was also known to spend hours afterwards just offering thanksgiving. Joseph couldn't quite remember the last time he spent a whole lot of time in thanksgiving. Mostly he felt that whatever time he spent in prayer was more of the pleading and asking kind.

Again, Joseph was perplexed by how this man's life was affecting his own. "Father in heaven, please accept my gratitude for all the ways you are in my life—for all the blessings you have given me in friends and family. Forgive me for having forgotten how much everything comes from Your hands. I solemnly promise to spend more time in gratitude in the days and years to come."

Joseph knew he wasn't expected to become like Sharbel; but he also knew that he could not read about this man's life and not be changed as well. Surely even a small change would be significant in God's eyes.

Here was a man who fought the good fight and Joseph vowed to become that same sort of man.

It was obvious to Joseph that Sharbel's superior had some sort of charism of prophecy because, as it turned out, he used some fairly accurate words to describe Sharbel. In the convent's registry he wrote:

> *On 24 December 1898, receiving the Sacraments of the Church, the hermit Father Sharbel Makhlouf of Bkkakafra was struck by paralysis. He was seventy. Because of what he will do after his death, I need not talk about his good behavior and, above all, the observance of his vows, and we may truly say that his obedience was more angelic than human.*

Incredible! In retrospect how could you have any other reaction to those words? Joseph wondered, as he looked at documentation on hundreds of miracles attributed to Sharbel's intercession. On top of that, apparently for forty-five nights after his death there was some sort of light surrounding his tomb; plus there were the crazy people who tried to steal his remains. Joseph was uncomfortable with this until he remembered his mother pointing out how people had brought their sick friends and family into the street just hoping that the apostle Peter's shadow would fall upon them and they would be healed. *Maybe there's something to all this,* Joseph admitted.

Joseph's attention went back to Sharbel as he read that when they finally opened the tomb they found Sharbel's incorrupt body floating in mud. This happened four months after he was buried so by anyone's standards it was pretty amazing. Incorrupt bodies—bodies that showed no sign of decay—were really significant in the Catholic Church; and rightfully so since very few people enjoyed that grace.

Two very specific miracles that led to Sharbel's beatification included the case of a woman—a Sister Maria Kamari—who had been suffering from a very painful ulcer. She had been operated on but the operation had failed. Her suffering continued for more than a decade in which she was bedridden and unable to eat without great difficulty. She was near death three specific times and was given last rites—a practice of Catholics wherein a person makes a last confession of sins and is sort of "prepared" to meet his or her maker. Joseph actually thought the practice was incredibly meaningful and knew that when the time came, he, too, would want something like that to help him meet his Creator.

Anyhow, Kamari's miracle occurred in 1950 which made it amazingly relevant to Joseph as this was the year his father was born. Kamari was taken to Sharbel's tomb in Annaya. She couldn't even walk on her own accord; but once there she spent a lot of time praying and actually felt her body get stronger. While she wasn't able to approach the tomb on her own, she was able to walk away from it without assistance. This caused many people to begin crying out that a miracle had been performed. She never had another problem after that healing.

While Joseph had been involved in the research, Miriam called. The phone startled him but when he saw it was Miriam, he quickly answered, "Shalom!"

"Shalom, Joseph! I had a few minutes of free time and wanted to check in on you. I was hoping you could come to Sabbath dinner."

A bit taken back by the invitation, Joseph nonetheless responded with enthusiasm, "I'd love to! Thank you!"

Miriam finished the call with details and Joseph then continued with his research.

The second of the Sharbel miracles was the instance of a man named Alessandro O'beid. After an accident in which the branch of a tree struck him, he lost sight from his right eye. The year was 1937. As was necessary for any miracle to be proclaimed, many doctors were involved and all their efforts remained unsuccessful. One doctor wrote the following:

> *According to science and conscience, we must say that an eye so ill and for so long was certainly lost forever. Therefore, we cannot explain how it has been cured, certainly not through natural means. We need to consider this extra-ordinary fact with great humility, and to attribute it to an Almighty will, which operates only by divine grace. There is no other explanation, and it is certain that we have seriously sought an explanation without finding one.*

Joseph read this and knew that in today's world of reason and knowledge; a willingness on the part of an "intellect" to give credit to God Almighty was just about a thing of the past. Not sure what that ultimately meant, Joseph continued to acknowledge that through the intercession of Sharbel, the man's sight was restored.

With such information, it was no wonder that people flocked to the site of his tomb seeking healing; simple people who believed in God and in His love for the world. *They will be our redemption,* Joseph thought. The world was, without a doubt, a very ill and wounded place. People suffered from ailments of the mind, body, and spirit. It would be the child-like—the simple people of faith—who would usher in God's kingdom.

Once the Sharbel miracles were confirmed, it was only a matter of time before his beatification. It took place in Rome on December 5, 1965. Certainly it was a momentous day for Catholics everywhere—as any such event is—but it must have been even more so for the Catholics of Lebanon. And as Joseph was now being told, it was becoming a place of discord as well. The tomb must remain in the hands of the holy. Joseph was beginning to really feel like he was fighting the good fight. He read the words of Pope Paul VI from the closing ceremony of the Second Vatican Council and was especially affected by certain parts of it:

> *These are, finally, the lessons derived from this ceremony for all. May St. Sharbel draw us after him along the path of sanctity, where silent prayer in the presence of God has its own particular place. May he make us understand, in a world largely fascinated by wealth and comfort, the paramount value of poverty, penance and asceticism, to liberate the soul in its ascent to God. The practice of these virtues is indeed different according to the various states of life and responsibilities of people. But no Christian can ignore them if he wants to follow Our Lord. These are the noble lessons, which Sharbel Makhlouf so timely gives us. That they may be well understood and practiced, We implore upon all, through the intercession of this new Blessed, already so venerated, an abundant effusion of graces; and paternally we bless you.*

Joseph was also moved by the October 9, 1977 canonization of Sharbel when Paul VI referred to the *Psalm 91:13*: The just will flourish like the palm tree and grow like a Lebanon cedar.

Joseph wasn't surprised to see that later on, in 1998, another pope—John Paul II—went on to beatify Father Nimitallah al-Hardini. As Joseph had discovered in learning about Sharbel, God planted people along each journey to help one another grow in holiness. Joseph quickly renewed his earlier promise to see each person God planted in his own life through the eyes of the Creator. Joseph did not want to miss any opportunities to be affected by those with whom he crossed paths—and to affect those with whom his path crossed. Joseph felt a longing in the depths of his heart and soul to serve God in a more substantial way.

Clearly, sainthood was a chance for everyone.

†

But first the Four Horsemen mission was before them with only Joseph knowing the full details and location.

Miriam and Joseph were both well aware that something like the Lebanon assignment was a real possibility in Joseph's future as a Mossad agent but nevertheless had allowed themselves to secretly dream of a different kind of life—a life where they became one and raised a family of their own, just like what he was witnessing right now. They had never shared this dream with each other; in fact, they had purposely kept it privately within their own hearts and danced around it. Maybe they were trying to protect one another, maybe they were trying to protect themselves; but tonight, somehow, Joseph knew it was a dream that they shared.

Not only would he need to tell Miriam of the Lebanon assignment, but he would have to profess his love for her—and hoped she would return that love. There were unquestionably more reasons for her to reject his love than to accept it and return it. Joseph knew with Miriam's loss of her mother in the horrendous bombing a few years ago, Miriam may well have decided—either consciously or subconsciously—it was better to keep her heart protected than to expose it to the possibility of more pain and anguish—which was a real possibility as the wife of a Mossad agent. Her time with the agency was almost up but Joseph's career would loom ahead of them always holding the unknown.

Miriam's hand lightly touched Joseph's sleeve and startled him out of his reverie and back to the present. "Joseph? Are you alright? You look very distant. Is everything okay?"

Joseph was always amazed at the complexity of this woman who stood next to him. He had watched and worked side-by-side as she had interrogated some of the most notorious terrorists Mossad had ever captured, gaining information that had saved countless lives. She was at once steel and silk. Miriam had a depth that few women Joseph had ever met possessed. She was brilliant and could decode messages more precisely than any agent in her group and yet for some time had been seemingly oblivious to the way in which Joseph had fallen so deeply in love with her. Even if the words were never spoken, surely everything about him seemed to scream how much he desired her heart. "Yes, yes, I'm fine. Just thinking about those nieces and nephews of mine. I haven't seen them in many months and I can only imagine how much they've grown. I admit, I miss Sarah and look forward to spending some time with her before…"

Joseph's sentence was cut short by the ringing phone which seemed to jump right out of its cradle. Miriam glanced backwards at Joseph even while she walked forward to answer it. The puzzled look on her face made Joseph realize what he had almost said …*before I go to Lebanon.* This had not been the time nor the place he wanted to share that information with Miriam.

"Shalom," Miriam greeted the caller. "Why yes, he is here. Just a moment and I'll get him." Quietly she said to Joseph, "That's odd. Why are you being called here and not on your cell?"

"Oh! I guess I wanted to have a few hours of quiet and figured if someone needed me and they had to make the additional effort to call your home then it must be important. That extra effort sort of weeded out unnecessary calls."

"Shalom," Joseph offered as he picked up the receiver. "Certainly. I understand." Looking at his watch he then added, "I will be there within the hour."

Chapter Six

So, whoever daily says, from his heart:
"Thy will be done," can confidently trust
that he will not fail to do God's will even
when he lacks actual certainty of it.

~ Edith Stein

Heading towards the door, Joseph simply said with a sheepish grin, "Give your father and brother my regards."

Miriam knew better than to question him on the mysterious phone call or where he was headed. *Why put either of us in an awkward position?* she thought to herself, knowing full well the life of a Mossad agent. "I will," was all she said and hugged Joseph as he made his way through the door jam, tenderly raising his hand to the mezuzah and silently asking for Adonai's protection.

The mezuzah was beautiful; it was made of stone. Ayala had purchased it a few weeks before her death. She had taken down the previous one and given it to David for his new home—she wanted him to know that she was always with him—just as the Creator was always present. It turned out to be a beautifully prophetic gesture that did not escape either David's attention or Miriam's, although neither brought it up.

That one was encased in silver. It had been a present from Meir's parents to Ayala and Meir when they had married. This new one was made of stone which seemed to reflect now, for Miriam at least, the strength that was her home and family—made of stone. It was affixed to the upper part of the door jamb as had been the silver one. The Hebrew letter Shin was at the center of the exterior of the small cylindrical shaped object since Shin was the representation of one of God's names: Shaddai—which means "all sufficient one." Most Jewish homes tended to follow the instructions found in the Torah which proclaimed that "The Great Commandment" should be posted on their doorposts— and worn on the arm and head. Miriam loved knowing that inside this relatively small—maybe 16x5 cm— cylinder, on kosher parchment paper, was written the words from Torah that lived in the hearts of all Jews:

> *Hear, O Israel! The Lord is our God, the Lord alone!*
> *Therefore, you shall love the Lord, your God, with all*
> *your heart, and with all your soul, and with all your*
> *strength. Take to heart these words which I enjoin on you*
> *today. Drill them into your children. Speak of them at*
> *home and abroad, whether you are busy or at rest. Bind*
> *them at your wrist as a sign and let them be as a pendant*
> *on your forehead. Write them on the doorposts of your*
> *houses and on your gates.*

This was why many orthodox Jewish men wore tefillin—the two black leather boxes containing the same words found in the mezuzah. Tefillin were tied onto the man's biceps and forehead with black leather straps. On occasion David had worn them and it had made both Ayala and Meir very proud to see him this way. Like all things in their faith, tefillin were rife with history and wearing them connected a Jewish man of today to God through obedience—and to countless men who had followed the same tradition for thousands of years.

Miriam had watched once as David attached the tefillin. They were tied on with special knots. One of them David wound seven times around his left forearm and hand. As he did this, he explained to Miriam it was because he was right handed. He said that someone who was left-handed would have tied it to their right forearm and hand. Miriam could feel David's love of their precious faith in his words as he explained what he was doing. He then attached the other box to his forehead right at the hairline. Its straps went around the back of his head, connecting at the top of his neck with that special knot.

The other Torah words that were in the mezuzah—and in the tefillin—that Joseph had so lovingly touched were similar:

> *If then, you truly heed my commandments which I enjoin on you today, loving and serving the Lord, your God, with all your heart and all your soul, I will give the seasonal rain, that you may have your grain, wine and oil to gather in; and I will bring forth grass in your fields for your animals. Thus you may eat your fill. But be careful lest your heart be so lured away that you serve other gods and worship them. For then the wrath of the Lord will flare up against you and he will close up the heavens, so that no rain will fall, and the soil will not yield its crops, and you will soon perish from the good land he is giving you.*

> *Therefore, take these words of mine into your heart and soul. Bind them at your wrist as a sign, and let them be a pendant on your forehead. Teach them to your children, speaking of them at home and abroad, whether you are busy or at rest. And write them on the doorposts of your houses and on your gates.*

Once back inside the apartment and with the front door closed, Miriam walked to the back door and let herself out onto the balcony. "Where's Joseph?" Meir asked as he peered through the open curtains trying to ascertain their guest's location.

"He's been called away on business and asked me to give you his regards."

"Just like that?" was David's response; but before that last syllable had been spoken, David understood. This was, after all, a time in which the nation's security was in great danger and each citizen was needed to carry a portion of the load. Joseph's might seem heavier than most but David was a great believer in prayer and felt that his own obligation to implore God, Blessed be His holy name, for Joseph's safe-keeping was also of paramount importance. Caring for one another in these ways was always a mitzvah.

Chapter Seven

Everyone, as his heart suggested and his spirit prompted, brought a contribution to the Lord

~ Exodus 35:21a

As Joseph made his way down the couple flights of stairs—bounding three at a time as he always accepted any chance for a physical challenge—from the Goldfarb apartment to the car waiting around the corner, he couldn't help but feel a sense of dread. As always, it was never for himself but more for his family and for Miriam. And his nation. No matter how war-torn or ravaged it became, it was his home. It was the home of his father and it was where Joseph and Sipporah were born. Joseph had very fond memories of his own childhood—never fully understanding what his mother gave up nor how brave it was for his father to bring home an American for a wife, let alone a Christian. That was the real reason that Mossad had so actively recruited Joseph: he was an anomaly with a Christian mother and a Jewish father. It wasn't that Joseph was a man without a country so much as he was a man with many loyalties and those loyalties could be used in Mossad's favor. Joseph spoke English, Hebrew and Arabic fluently. His French was hit-or-miss but could get him by in a pinch. Indeed, had gotten him by in a pinch. And he really loved God—even if the Almighty seemed a bit distant, or unknowable. What he had gained from his unique childhood was that God was the God of Abraham, Isaac, Jacob, and Joseph, his own namesake. The God of the Jews was the same God of the Christians. And that became the strong, sure foundation upon which his parents built their home and marriage.

"Shalom aleichem," Joseph said to the driver as the passenger door closed.

"Aleichem shalom," was the response. After all, the driver was well aware of the mission awaiting Joseph and most certainly meant it when he said "unto you peace."

They continued their conversation in French, but had always greeted one another in the common Hebrew greeting of peace. For many people, this was simply a habit, a formality; but, for these agents, the words held sincerity that was an almost sacred hope that having been uttered, Adonai would honor the peace offering and keep the friends out of harm's way. In fact, this greeting of peace was taken so seriously that a rabbi once said that if a person offered "peace unto you" and was not met with the response "unto you peace," then the person was considered robbed. There had been a time when Joseph would sometimes simply nod and smile when someone offered him a greeting of peace; but upon learning what this rabbi taught, he always made a point to respond whenever someone offered him peace.

"This happened quicker than I had expected. What changed the timeline?"

"Well, for one thing, there seems to have been a leak of information. It is still undetermined who is responsible but the leak has forced the hand of the government. They now need to make their move or lose the last two years of intel."

"A leak? How can that be?" Joseph shuddered to think of the dangerous position this put the project in.

The dangerous position it put Miriam in! "Do the operatives know?"

"They don't. The decision was made that it would be safer for everyone to go ahead as planned. There can be no more interruptions, no more hesitations. The meeting is to proceed."

The summit that Aadil spoke of was the secret gathering that included the pope, the highest Muslim cleric in Lebanon, and the two chief rabbis in Israel. For the purpose of the mission the meeting's participants were given code names: White Dove, Aayan, Abdas and Abdeel. Selecting the names for the men was both a job and an honor. For most people of Middle Eastern descent, a name is so much more than a mere label. For the agents assigned to the task of covertly securing a meeting location and acting as go-betweens for the four dignitaries, the names assigned were to give respect and pay tribute to each man's own unique religious role for his people.

The pope was named "White Dove" in deference to the ways in which he was said to be guided by the Holy Spirit, often seen as a white dove. The Muslim cleric was named "Aayan" which refers to a "notable person" or "God's gift." While some of the Muslim faith preferred to reserve this name in the most sacred sense for God alone, the team determined that they used the title as more of an honor and not in trying to undermine or in any way usurp God's ultimate reign and authority. The rabbis, one Sephardic and the other Ashkenazi, were given different forms of the name which means "servant of God:" Abdas and Abdeel.

The operation itself was decidedly called "Four Horsemen" because these four holy men were seen as the antithesis of each horsemen in Scripture. Everyone involved in the mission recognized that if there was to be any way in which the world could change its course, and avoid an apocalypse—whether the one foretold in the holy books or simply the one taking place through the degradation of humans through society's current obsession with self aggrandizement and narcissism, it would be through the words and actions of these four men.

The first horseman of the apocalypse is said to be intent on conquest and is often seen as the anti-Christ. According to end-time scholars, this horseman will overthrow all who get in his way. He will take no prisoners. White Dove was his antithesis.

The second horseman will be able to take peace from people and cause men to kill one another. This horseman becomes the catalyst for complete warfare among humankind. Aayan was his antithesis.

The third horseman brings famine—often seen as a result of the warfare ushered in by the second horseman while the fourth horseman is the completion of the previous horsemen and is death and destruction. The antithesis of these two horsemen existed in the two rabbis that were part of the mission: code names Abdas and Abdeel.

All the agents knew, full well, that their respective charges—White Dove, Aayan, Abdas and Abdeel—had the ability to change world events, to even avoid what looked to many observers to be the end of days—to stem the tide of death and destruction that was currently covering the planet.

Chapter Eight

*But even the unlearned perceive how
ridiculous it is to suppose that
instruments are moved, unless they are set
in motion by some principal agent.*

*This would be like fancying that, when a
chest or a bed is being built, the saw or the
hatchet performs its functions without the
carpenter. Accordingly, there must be a
first mover that is above all the rest; and
this being we call God.*

~ St. Thomas Aquinas

While Joseph was well aware of Miriam's role in the Four Horsemen operation, Miriam was completely unaware of Joseph's. Because the lines of their personal and professional relationship were clear, the two never discussed the other's work life without an invitation to do so—and the invitations were never forthcoming from either party.

As Miriam finished enjoying her coffee and compote with her father and her brother, the phone in the apartment rang again. "My, aren't we popular this Sabbath evening," Meir remarked as he walked inside to lift the phone from its cradle. "Shalom," was all he said before the caller queried as to Miriam's availability. Meir was used to completing his greeting with "Goldfarb residence" but the urgency of the call seemed to rise right up from the phone wires and Meir did not hesitate to motion to Miriam through the glass window to take the call.

"Miriam Goldfarb here," was all she said before she began simply nodding her head in agreement as if the caller could see her affirmation. After a fairly quick two-minute conversation, Miriam replaced the phone in its cradle and gave her father a hug. "Abba, I have to leave now." Seeing the alarmed look on her father's face, despite his efforts to hide it, she quickly added, "Everything is all right. Let me go give David a hug and I'll be on my way."

Just as Miriam and Joseph respected one another's privacy in all things related to work, so, too, did Miriam's father and brother understand that Miriam would never be able to reveal what she did, or needed to do, and there was no reason to put her in a situation in which she would be forced to lie to those whom she loved so deeply.

"May Adonai, Blessed be His holy name, watch over you and keep you safe," were the words that David issued to his sister. His father watched helplessly as Miriam departed. Meir smiled at Miriam and gave a slight inclination to her with his head as if to say, *You are my beloved daughter and I hold you always in my heart.*

Miriam knew full well the ache that her father felt as it was the same ache she was doing her best to squelch at Joseph's departure just moments before her own. She wondered if Joseph had any idea how she felt about him—or if he had feelings for her.

Within minutes of closing the door to the apartment, Miriam was seated in the back seat of a dark sedan very much like the one that had driven Joseph away. The stars in the sky continued to twinkle and the clouds continued to dance to their destiny. As she closed the door Miriam heard the driver murmur "Shalom."

"Shalom."

"Forgive me if I don't exchange pleasantries but I have been asked to brief you as quickly and thoroughly as possible before we arrive at Ben Gurion Airport." Miriam's father did not live far from the well-known international airport that was named after the Israeli statesman David Ben Gurion, the first prime minster of Israel. Miriam simply nodded her head, once again, in understanding and agreement.

The driver continued with bone-chilling words, "The operation has been compromised."

Miriam shivered despite the warm temperature and saw, but did not feel, that her hand had gripped the edge of the seat. She had long ago learned how to separate her mind from her circumstances as a means of survival but there would always be the natural responses rendered because of her own humanity. That fleeting moment when the body's autonomic response of fight or flight was in charge before her mind could wrestle control of a situation. As a Mossad agent, that time between the natural physiological response and the ability to get it under control was almost negligible, but there it was, rearing its ugly head before Miriam willed herself to release her vice-like grip on the edge of the seat.

"To answer your unspoken question," the driver continued, "no, we do not know who or how the operation was compromised. It was chatter picked up from sources who we have always found to be reliable in the ways that bragging can bring out the truth in any terrorist situation.

"Right now your private flight to the meeting has been secured. I will drop you off at the tarmac of a private jet and you will be delivered to a location only known to the senior agents. The plane will have your most recent 'go-bag' on board and all other items necessary have been placed in the front pocket of the bag."

Miriam knew this meant that her undercover identity as a citizen in whatever country she was being delivered to would be part of the "other items" of which the driver spoke. "Do you know how many other agents will be on board?"

"Due to the secrecy of this operation, there will only be three agents along with you. I have not been cleared to know who they will be but have been told to let you know that you will be accompanied by three additional personnel."

Miriam looked out the window of the sedan, seeing Sabbath candles lit in apartment windows, and prayed that the mission would be a success. She only knew her role in it and couldn't help but feel a quickening of her pulse when she thought about having to protect the White Dove.

Chapter Nine

Now we are about to begin and you must attend!

And when we get to the end of the story, you will know more than you do now about a very wicked hobgoblin.

He was one of the worst kind; in fact he was a real demon.

~ Hans Christian Andersen

It is often difficult to tell, once things come to fruition, how or where they all began. As each agent made his or her way to Ben Gurion Airport in a dark sedan, each being briefed about the intelligence leak, there was also a calm that descended upon the individuals in the elite group. They had been planning this for quite a while and felt eager anticipation that the time had finally arrived; but there was also an imposing sense of fate or destiny that couldn't be ignored.

Where this operation began was just about anybody's guess—each agent assuming the other was in possession of more details but knowing better than to "compare notes." Loyalty to country, to fellow agents, and to family all came after loyalty to God. And all agents in the operation believed fully that God was to be best served in the days that lie ahead, regardless of what they held. No one denied that God was known to deliver punishment just as often as He delivered mercy. Theirs was not to question which they would be receiving but to trust in God with, literally, their lives and the lives of many others.

The world teetered on the very brink of destruction. People who claimed that God did not exist seemed to have a lot of evidence to support their views. Warring factions claimed every corner of the world. Economies were crumbling and nothing could stop the bleed; measures attempted to do so only made matters worse. Weather systems ravaged the globe; hurricanes, tornadoes, floods, and fires wiped out tens of thousands of people while the rest of the world watched in horror—or indifference. Biological warfare appeared imminent, only to be outdone by man's own ability to inflict harm upon fellow man. One man's religion was seen as another man's reason to hate. Co-existence seemed completely impossible. Gestures that were made at peace were seen as grand but empty. *Who would be willing to make the first move? What would it take for people to truly change?* Miriam often wondered.

Each agent pondered the same sort of questions and then, just as quietly as he or she had been whisked away into the quiet Sabbath evening, each was boarding the plane, destination unknown.

Being the first called, as head of the team, Joseph was the initial agent on the plane. He stood at the rear, facing the short aisle so that as each agent boarded, he or she was greeted with a nod and a gesture indicating which seat to take.

Abdul was the first on the plane, after Joseph. Like the other agents that would follow, Abdul masked his surprise at seeing Joseph and simply sat in the designated seat after picking up the folder that was located on the dark blue cushion. Abdul was from Lebanon and loved his beautiful homeland with Jabal Al-gharb—often simply called "Mt. Lebanon"—stretching the entire length of the country, running parallel to the Mediterranean Sea with its northern portion extending right into Syria. Abdul's heart ached when he thought of how greatly Lebanon had suffered over the years and the sad reality that the country had even been used as a battlefield for different powers within the region. Lebanon gained its independence from the French in 1943 but its history was marred by a bloody civil war that began in the mid 70s and ended in the early 90s. Too much bloodshed had made Abdul responsive to the request to join the international group who would become the guardians of the Four Horsemen.

Abdul's job was simple: protect Aayan, the Muslim cleric.

Next on board was Joffa. Joffa grew up on the streets on Jerusalem and was often found helping his father in the marketplace. His father was an amiable man, only wanting to earn a fair living selling his goods. Joffa and Miriam were the same age and unbeknownst to either, both were at the marketplace that horrible day when the bomb exploded that took the life of Miriam's mother, Ayala. At the time Miriam's family had a guest, an American woman named Elizabeth. All had spent the day at the marketplace and it pained Joffa to know that this American had experienced the horror of hate and terror firsthand.

For Joffa, that fateful day was when all the lines between friends and foes evaporated. Arab and Jew alike were killed in the explosion. Faith did not keep anyone safe and Muslims as well as Christians and Jews died hideous deaths as the explosion rocked the marketplace. The sight of it all—the blood, the severed limbs—amidst the sounds of screaming and sirens forever changed Joffa. He became an easy sell when approached to join the elite team of international brokers that were to escort four men from different corners of the world who, on the face of it, seemed as diverse as night and day; but were, in reality, all seeking the same thing: peace for their people. Joffa's job in this operation: protect Abdas and Abdeel, the two rabbis.

When Miriam boarded the jet, Joseph was flipping through a few pages of notes and didn't immediately notice her arrival. It was her gasp, quickly covered up, that got his attention. Torn between wanting to run to him and disappear into this arms and needing to find a seat to steady her nerves, Miriam took the first seat to her left. As it wasn't a designated seat, it had no folder thus forcing Joseph to move down the short aisle to the seat he had intended for her and pick up the folder and walk it over to her. Neither of them wanted to risk exchanging greetings—not confident that emotions wouldn't be betrayed by their voices. Of course Joseph knew to expect Miriam and so his emotional condition was more electrified by the mere knowledge that the one he deeply loved was in very real jeopardy; Miriam's was the full surprise that the covert operation had been masterminded by Joseph. She had always known the day would come when she would know who had been able to pull all of this together but had never suspected it would be Joseph.

Chapter Ten

A woman's way to holiness is clearly to
purify her God-given sensitivity and to
direct it into the proper channels.

~ Alice von Hildebrand

With all agents aboard the Lockheed SR-71 Blackbird, Joseph quickly took the opportunity to answer what he knew to be the burning question on everyone's mind, "It was as surprising to me as it must have been to each of you to find out that our mission has been compromised. Since finding out about that less than an hour ago, I've been able to discover that the leak came from within the ranks."

Joseph let the audible gasps evaporate before he continued, "One of the agents—all of whom had been vetted to the fullest degree—was willing to sell the details of the mission to the highest bidder. From what we can now tell, the information was sold in increments to a number of different governments and terrorist groups all wanting to put an end to this mission of peace. What that means is that up to five different organizations are in possession of bits and pieces of information. That works in our favor—but only if we begin now. Current intel indicates a possible bomb will be used with a number of these different organizations participating in its explosion. Decoys are expected to be set up by one group while another sets up a sharp-shooter. We can't rely on this information completely but it gives us a starting point. This is why you've all been summoned and our mission is currently underway."

As Joseph continued, the agents were all told that each of their charges was being picked up and delivered to the secret location. The agents were then asked to read through the contents of their folders and to be prepared to engage the moment the Blackbird landed.

Chapter Eleven

*That's why the time to prepare for life's
disappointments and hurts is in advance,
before they come crashing down upon us.*

~ Billy Graham

Elizabeth and Luke were celebrating their 30th wedding anniversary at their favorite restaurant when Luke handed Elizabeth a rather large envelope. They had been through a lot together in their 30 years of marriage. Like any couple, they had experienced both ups and down in their lives and in the raising of their children—now all grown and essentially out on their own. There were times when Elizabeth had been overwhelmed by the responsibility of her family. She and Luke never seemed to agree on anything and each day brought new ways to hurt one another. While it was never fully intentional, it was painful nonetheless. And in the middle of the pain was also great joy and many fond memories, no doubt gifts from God to keep Elizabeth and Luke connected.

Wistfully, Beth—as Luke called her—realized that this was really what marriage was all about: a very long race in which the grand prize was somehow bittersweet. Lessons learned made your heart ache to take back time and get a "do-over" as so many movies popularized; but those same lessons made the journey precious and fruitful. Beth wondered if you could get to the depths of love without the ups and downs that preceded it and decided that you probably couldn't.

Now, their daughter Sophia was getting married and the boys were each diving into life—head first as was their typical approach to everything—and enjoying every minute of it. Beth wanted so much to have a do-over that she had to often force herself to stop looking back. *What good does it do?* she would chide herself when the melancholy of the moment would be too much to bear.

It was in her nature to withdraw to her own world of prayer and quiet and if it hadn't been for her husband's love and commitment—even the "tough love" moments—Beth wondered if she would just have drawn the blinds and lived the life of a hermit.

"Well?" Luke chimed into Elizabeth's thoughts. "Are you going to open it or do you think through osmosis you'll figure out what's inside?"

Beth laughed and thought how in their early years of marriage those words would have felt harsh and her response would have been to sulk and possibly return the envelope to Luke without any interest in its contents. But now Beth said dryly, "I wasn't going for osmosis as much as I was trying out my x-ray vision."

Both chuckled, each knowing how far they had come in their decades together. Tugging at the sealed envelope, Elizabeth's interest was truly piqued. *Could it be tickets to the concert she had wanted to see? Might he be giving her a note and a promise to replace the well-worn couch in the front room?*

None of Beth's imaginings prepared her for what was held inside and with a shout that startled the clientele at the nearby tables, Elizabeth jumped from her seat and then quietly implored, "Italy? We're going to Italy?"

The sparkle in Luke's eyes said it all: *Yes, my love, we are going to Italy.*

With no verbal response from Luke, but not needing one, Beth sat down, leaned over and hugged him. It was a hug that encompassed the widest range of emotions possible. Elizabeth was filled with gratitude that didn't arrive from the gift of the trip—although she was sure that would be another layer at another point in time—but from the realization of how much Luke had grown in his efforts to "know" her. Beth had pilgrimaged alone to Israel and had voiced that the only other trip she truly wanted to take in her lifetime was to Italy. He had paid attention and that was what filled her with gratitude. She also felt a deep sense of commitment to Luke. One that had grown over the years and because of the two-steps-forward-one-step-back life they had lived. What Elizabeth had come to understand was that even if every two steps forward resulted in one step back, you still moved forward! Painful and tedious as it may sometimes feel, the momentum was undeniably there. God allowed her to see it every day in a number of small, seemingly inconsequential ways; but allow her to see it, He did.

Chapter Twelve

*When a man is at home, the Zohar says,
he should maintain good relations with his
wife.*

*In this way he creates the balanced,
harmonious, and altogether complete
environment in which the divine
presence—the Shekinah—can
comfortably reside.*

~ Rav Berg

"The White Dove is secure," was all that the message relayed. The assumption would obviously be that the White Dove was where he should be and the agent was simply awaiting further instructions.

Miriam's flight—the flight that included Abdul, Joffa and Joseph—had arrived in parts unknown in the expected time frame: less than 3 hours. Miriam, like the other agents, was unaware of where they were headed, but wasn't surprised that it was Italy. This wasn't her first trip to the country as the Four Horsemen mission required numerous reconnaissance flights in which she had to run a number of options from start to finish in preparation for this day. Along with Italy, those same options were also run in Turkey, Japan, and South America. However, if Miriam had been a betting woman—which she was not—her money would have been on a location somewhere in the Pacific Remote Islands. It seemed a bit odd to her that the pope's own territory would be where the mission was deemed safest. Of course there was always that old adage "hidden in plain sight" that was now coming to mind and Miriam had to admit that old adages became such due to the truths that existed within them.

So it was that Miriam began her three-day excursion around Rome playing the role of a tourist to the hilt. And she had to admit that there was so much about the ancient city that captured her attention, in some ways her "acting" had more realism in it then did a true tourist's reaction to the city. She chalked this up to the fact that multiple trips to Rome had provided an opportunity for her to truly take in each site in its glory instead of feeling a need to rush from one location to another, as tourists often do, and then rely on photographs taken to recall this site or that attraction.

By far, Miriam found the hustle and bustle of Rome to be what affected her most. It reminded her of home: merchants lining the aged pathways with their wares, people were often shoulder to shoulder as they made their way around the winding streets searching for the perfect café from which to sit and enjoy a cup of espresso or a delicious gelato dessert. Kids running. People laughing.

Sights and sounds and smells could transport you to a time and a place and that is what Rome did for Miriam: it transported her to her days as a young teenager walking the streets of Tel Aviv or Jerusalem, loving her city, loving her life.

Now, 20 some odd years later, Miriam was a Mossad agent commissioned with protecting the pope, the man who, according to the billion plus Catholics, was the successor of Peter, a Jewish man. Every time Miriam thought about this, she was filled with wonder and awe. How did a few Jewish guys start up a whole new way to connect with God? Walking the streets of Rome did that to a person: it made you contemplate the very big issues of history and the connection between those who believed Jesus was the son of God—the long awaited Messiah—and those who believed the Messiah was still to come.

Miriam's first day in Rome would include the Trevi fountain where Miriam would, like all the other tourists, throw coins into the structure where the hope—or wish—was that there would be a return trip to Rome. So far, Miriam had to admit that it seemed to be working. She pushed her way past the throngs of people and tossed her coins into the baroque fountain. Its lavishness still astounding her. She remembered quite distinctly returning from her first trip to Rome and researching everything she could about the city and the artists who built it, who were—in some cases—required to work for the church, but who all had left in indelible mark upon the city and whose work still impacted thousands upon thousands of people a year.

It was rather amazing to stand, now, at the fountain of Trevi; located at the end of an aqueduct which itself was constructed before the Jewish man Jesus was born. Apparently at one point, Pope Urban VIII had commissioned the great artist Bernini to design just such a fountain but that effort came to an end with the pope's death. A hundred years later, another pope, Clement XII, made a commissioning of his own and Nicola Salvi created what became the most spectacular fountain in all of Rome.

The size alone mesmerized Miriam as it is said to measure 26 meters in height and that the statue of Neptune in the center measures almost six meters in height.

Standing there, Miriam allowed the rich symbolism to capture her imagination. There was Neptune, holding a cloth to cover his nudity, on a chariot that was being pulled by two tritons. One was tranquil and the other agitated, the combination is said to represent, and rightfully so, the different qualities of the ocean.

Miriam understood symbolism. She thought of the Sabbath candles that her mother would light as symbolically welcoming God's light into the Jewish home on Friday evening. Miriam knew that this was the single most significant way the Sabbath was ushered in and couldn't help but feel a deep sense of connection to Sarah, the wife of Abraham, who was the first Jewish woman to perform this mitzvah—this good deed—of lighting Sabbath candles. Miriam was filled with a deep longing to spend just one more Sabbath dinner with her own mother, Ayala. When she closed her eyes, Miriam could see her mother lighting the candles and could hear her mother chant the Sabbath prayers.

Yes, symbolism made life richer and endeared a person to her ancestors in a very special way. Miriam prayed that God would bless her with her own children one day and that she would be able to pass on the tradition of Sabbath dinners and lighting candles.

†

The first day in Rome was also the day Miriam was designated to visit the Colosseum. The Colosseum was made from the same travertine stone that was used to build the fountain. Miriam chuckled and wondered how many Americans knew that the famous Getty Center in California was made from travertine that was imported from Tivoli quarries that supplied stone to these ancient structures. Very few people, Miriam mused, cared about history. *Maybe that is why,* she ruminated, *people are far too willing to move ahead and forget the past.* For her the past is what made her fully alive in the here-and-now; it was all about knowing how she was connected to others that gave her life hope and purpose—and the idea that one day she would pass on that heritage to children of her own made her heart skip a beat and brought a picture of Joseph to mind.

She prayed he was safe.

Once they had landed each agent immediately went his or her separate way as the planned operation began. None knowing the other's designated agenda for their divided time; only knowing the predetermined times and locations of their joint meetings.

With her mind back on the task at hand, Miriam marveled at the difference a bit of information made for her as she now stood in front of the Colosseum. Her eyes saw it with new understanding, an understanding that left her saddened and yet quizzical.

So much horror and pain took place within the Colosseum walls—and yet so much honor.

On her first trip, the structure—which was severely decayed from age and weather—simply represented some sort of arena where people gathered to watch "games." Now, armed with information gained from intense research, she found herself crying for all the people who had come to believe in this man, Jesus, and who had lost their lives for that belief. Instead of recanting, they often seemed to look for ways to die for this Jewish man who spoke in parables and talked of things like heaven and hell. They offered their lives to proclaim that he was the long-awaited Messiah!

She couldn't make sense of it. She kept thinking, *If he was the Messiah, why did he allow all these people to die? And not just death but horrifically, in some of the most inhumane ways possible. What kind of Messiah was that?*

This was why, Miriam knew, many Jews did not believe. They couldn't reconcile the fact that the long-awaited Messiah did not change the human condition;

and, in fact, sometimes the human condition was made worse for believing in him.

Miriam shook herself out of her morose thinking and continued on with the scheduled stops of her first day. As the evening began to roll in, she wound her way back to her hotel—a converted hospital that still had a bit of an antiseptic feel to it, although it worked well enough as it provided a place to shower and sleep. Miriam always found that when on these types of missions, her appetite was less than ravenous; she ate out of necessity, not out of desire.

Chapter Thirteen

*God is not passively enduring the ways
and wisdom of this world; He is in violent
opposition to the wisdom of this world.*

~ Corey Russell

Beth was well prepared for the flight to Italy, having learned from her trip to Israel that sleeping on the flight was an important first step towards a successful first day—and beyond. She brought with her a number of items including a small neck pillow and an eye mask. All in all, she felt ready to catch a few winks once the dinner trays were removed.

Luke, on the other hand, was a bundle of nerves. Elizabeth thought this was rather ironic since Luke travelled often on business and had certainly been to a number of other countries—although never to Italy. In some sweet way, Beth felt her husband was acting like a moonstruck young college boy trying to ask the president of a sorority out, or some such thing. She could see that Luke felt there was a lot riding on this trip—and maybe he was right, she wasn't exactly sure. What she did know was that the gesture itself had won her over. It was the next set of "two steps forward" and she just tried to ignore the "one step back" feeling that played over and over again in the back of her mind.

Since returning from Israel where Elizabeth found the God of her hopes and dreams, the God of her joy and peace, she had also begun pursuing spiritual direction. Luke let her do this without even so much as peep. Not a single syllable questioning what, exactly, spiritual direction was or why she needed it. There was a time when this would have made Luke squirm in discomfort imagining that all the household and family secrets would be revealed. That was a silly response, of course, but that was her Luke. So when he seemed to understand that this was something she wanted to do, he gave his blessings in his own, silent way.

And she appreciated that gesture, like this trip, more than he could possibly know.

Her time in Israel taught her to enjoy who she was and not strive to be someone else. The ship had sailed on all the ways she had long ago envisioned her life; but that didn't mean she still wasn't on a great journey! Elizabeth instinctively knew that she had to stop reading so many fiction novels where everything seemed perfect and the husband and wife were completely compatible and the kids were, well, semi-robots. She had to stop visiting websites and blogs where the perfect wives talked about their perfect husbands and their ideal kids—or where their "confessions" about their imperfections were less than honest and more for show.

Although the appeal of such an existence never fully went away, the ability to live in the life she was given grew by leaps and bounds while she was in the Holy Land. And for that she was incredibly thankful.

It was her spiritual director who helped her quell the voices in the back of her mind, the ones that said, "Okay, now that you've taken two steps forward, be prepared for one step back." The dreadful voices that could so easily rob her of her joy were finally taking a back seat to the truths of her life as a beloved daughter of God—or Abba as she began calling him after her trip to the Holy Land.

Of course none of this happened without struggle, but the struggle was well worth it. Being able to breathe deep, as it were, and not get the breath caught in her throat was a whole new way of living. Beth fondly recalled the Blessing of the Throat Mass she recently attended. It was on the feast day of St. Blaise who is reported to have saved a young boy from chocking to death and then had performed many other miracles. The blessing that Beth received was a beautiful experience, rife with symbolism as the priest blessed two candles and then crossed those candles at the base of Beth's throat and prayed:

> *Saint Blaise, pray for us that we may not suffer from illnesses of the throat and pray that all who are suffering be healed by God's love. Amen*

Beth recognized that blessing as a way to begin speaking truths to herself and to more fully step into what her spiritual director often said to her: "It is time for you to learn to 'be.'"

Beth liked the idea of "be-ing" and speaking truths to herself.

Chapter Fourteen

*In their old age, our great-grandparents
lived in great poverty, but they still
managed to spare some of what they had
for those who were even poorer.*

~ Edith Stein

Miriam's second day in Italy was as enjoyable as her first. All agents assigned to this case were to spend this day sight-seeing as well. If any of them were being followed, an additional day of touring Rome would make their cover air-tight; they seemed nothing more than typical tourists to any observer. For Miriam, this day included a trip to the Sistine Chapel, the Pieta, and the Spanish Steps. History, again, was Miriam's closest friend.

Who wasn't captivated by the story of Michelangelo lying on his back for years to paint what would become one of the most famous artworks ever? And in the 1500s no less! Miriam chuckled when she thought about the arrogance of the current age. She knew that everyone believed that this age was the best, most advanced age. And yet Rome reminded anyone who was paying attention that this really wasn't an assumption that one could honestly make. Consider the structure of the Colosseum or the aqueduct system. It wasn't about the time you were living in as much as what you were doing with your life in the age in which you lived. Walking towards the Sistine Chapel, Miriam chuckled again. Maybe the heat was a bit too much because she was now talking to herself and seemingly talking in circles to boot. She fondly recalled Elizabeth, her American friend, and some of what Elizabeth had shared about the "conversations" she had in head. They could be exhausting, that was for sure.

Miriam's ticket to the Sistine Chapel allowed her to sidestep the crowds and take place in a line that was quickly moving inside. Once inside, Miriam knew that while she loved all of Michelangelo's work, the tapestries that lined the walls of the Vatican Museum had really become her favorite pieces to look at as she marveled at the artistry involved and imagined all the people who had walked upon the carpets when they were considered nothing more than "rugs" or something to cover the floors. Those tapestries depicted a wide variety of scenes from everyday life to royalty— each more detailed and breath-taking than the last. Miriam particularly loved, just as she did when she gazed upon the sculpture of David or the many pieces of art that were physically massive, how an artist could envision the whole thing and then step back and tackle it piece by piece; brush stroke by brush stroke; thread by thread—whatever the case may be. She remembered her meager attempts at painting once when she ran out of canvas before she completed her landscape scene. Clearly she was not in command of the talents to see the big picture and then know how to go about attaining it.

The mission that was before her had the same precision to it: first the big picture was determined— sketched out as it were—and then all the pieces were put into play. She was proud that Joseph had such skills and knew his passions were just as valuable. Thinking of him, she realized that she was ready to admit that she loved him truly and deeply; but was he ready to hear it?

Miriam really had no idea how Joseph felt about her.

†

Miriam's second day in Rome went just as was expected. She enjoyed her time at the Sistine Chapel and then marveled at the Pieta where, once again, she stood motionless as she tried to imagine the pain of the woman who held her beloved, dead son in her arms. A Jewish mother, a Jewish son.

Her final stop of the day was the infamous Spanish Steps in the northern part of the city next to Piazaa Trinità dei Monti. Everyone who traveled to Rome made a point of walking the steps—even if unable to climb them in their entirety as they were, after all, the most expansive set of stairs in all of Europe. Miriam always made a point of climbing them with a two-fold purpose in mind. First, every chance she had to keep in shape, she took. Staying in top physical form was part of her requirements as an agent and she knew would always prove valuable in any sort of extreme situation. Second, and maybe more importantly right now, Miriam used the opportunity to take in the surroundings without appearing to be looking for anything in particular.

According to the documents she read through on the flight from Israel to Italy, Miriam would be confirmed for her third and final day's duties for the Four Horsemen assignment by climbing the Spanish Steps at the end of her second day and looking out upon the square and observing a woman with a red scarf tied to her waist in deep conversation with another woman wearing a red pair of shoes.

After walking the steps, taking in the grandeur of the surrounding buildings, and with the Trinità dei Monti church in sight, Miriam spotted her confirmation and found herself saying a brief prayer.

It was on.

The mission was a go.

Her first thoughts were to ask for Hashem's guidance and protection for what would be—without question—a moment that could change the entire trajectory of the world as it was known.

It seemed like such a grand statement to be thought by such an inconsequential woman.

Chapter Fifteen

Therefore becoming is properly predicated of the rational soul. Since the soul is not composed of matter and form, as was shown above, it cannot be brought into being except by creation. But God alone can create, as we said above. Consequently the rational soul is produced by God alone.

~ St. Thomas Aquinas

Elizabeth and Luke landed safely in Rome. Luke's painstaking attention to detail made all their accommodations easy and successful. Once they claimed their baggage and had cleared customs, which to Beth's dismay included an almost invisible stamp on their passports, they were met by the driver whose broken English informed them that they were just a quick ride to the small apartment they had rented for the week.

Unfortunately, the trip to the apartment in the small sports car seemed more adventurous than Beth was up to because even though she had slept—however fitfully—on the plane, she still felt overcome with exhaustion. Things were catching up to her: the emotions of it all, the flight, even her hungry stomach was sounding alarms. Oddly, the stamped passport was the thing that seemed to be setting her over the edge. *Just my luck*, she thought to herself, *the one time I will be in Italy and they can't have a fresh ink pad so that the stamp shows up on my passport!*

Trying to shake herself free from the feelings that wanted to trap her and steal her joy, she closed the passport with a resounding clap of pages and took Luke's hand in her own. No words needed to be exchanged and they just looked out their windows enjoying the beauty of the day and the magnificence of the city.

A bit of humidity hung in the air but it was still a refreshing change from the stale air on the plane. The sun shone and the surroundings staked a claim on Beth's heart and soul. She felt Luke gently squeeze her hand and knew he felt the same way. If they weren't careening around roads and ducking in and out of traffic lanes, it would have been if they had stepped back in time. The buildings—if such a word could be used to describe the structures—were each more magnificent than the last. Gazing at the reliefs of gargoyles and saints and martyrs adorning structures whose intricacy belied a craftsmanship unlike few others, both Beth and Luke were transfixed. Their mingled fingers pulsing with a love that had been built up, over the years, just as the buildings they were passing had been: there was work and struggle but there was also passion and a knowing of what to do that arises out of a deep intimacy and knowledge. A stone-cutter would intimately use his tools to craft a statue while a husband and wife would intimately use the experiences of their lives to craft their marriage.

After arriving at their destination, Luke retrieved the suitcases from the car and placed them at the apartment's entrance. Beth grabbed the handle of hers and headed inside while Luke paid the driver and confirmed their departure day and time for which the driver would clearly be taking them back to the airport. The prospect of a week of time free and clear of any demands seemed more exciting than what the day held, which was to head to St. Peter's Square.

Luke's research into rental apartments proved fruitful and both Beth and Luke were pleasantly surprised when they opened the door to what would be "home" for the next week. As much as they wanted to tour the city—and had no plans other than to stay in Rome—they also knew they were "homebodies" and that wherever they were staying needed to be a welcome retreat from whatever the day would hold. This is where they would enjoy each other's company and would retire to relive the day's adventures.

It was perfect.

The apartment, though small, maybe only 600 or 700 square feet, had all the amenities that they needed. It was two flights of stairs up and had a small balcony off the main room which itself held an inviting couch, a small side chair, and a galley kitchen. The one bedroom and bathroom were each located off the main area. The bedroom held an adequate-sized bed with a quilt covering it. It was flanked by two small dressers that were meant to also serve as night stands. Each had a lamp with a shade that picked up the rose hues from the quilt. Beth loved the fringe around the shades and felt immediately at home in the room. It may have been sparsely furnished but it matched the way she felt: simple and yet complete.

The bathroom was more of the same in that it was neither too much nor too little. While it did not entice one to indulge in a spa-like experience, neither was it lacking anything would make their stay less than comfortable. The shower stall was large enough for a relaxed shower but there was no tub. Beth remembered lounging in the tub during her trip to the Holy Land and while it would have been nice to be able to do the same here, she didn't feel like she would be missing anything if she didn't unwind in a tub this week.

Nowhere in the apartment was there a television set. Unlike her acceptance of no tub, the lack of a television made Beth wince. Luke caught her subtle, yet discernable, reaction of dismay and immediately decided to reassure her each day did not need to end with yet another episode of some mindless sitcom or watching the news. Beth was placated and happily grabbed her suitcase and rolled it into the bedroom.

Luke followed with his and both silently began unpacking and settling in. Creatures of habit made each want to feel organized before starting the day. It didn't take long and was close to lunch time when the bathroom items had been put in place and Luke announced, "Okay, it's time for our 'Roman Holiday' to begin!"

Beth laughed as she recalled that at home, in preparation for the trip, they had decided to rent a few Rome-related movies and one of their favorites had been *Roman Holiday*. The other was *Return to Me* which they watched twice because it had everything they liked in a movie: humor, love, triumph.

"Should we change or shower?"

"I'm fine," Luke answered, clearly ready to begin his 'Roman Holiday' and then grabbed the apartment keys off the counter.

"Okay, then, let's go!" was Beth's eager response.

Their plan was to spend each of their days roaming the city, waiting in lines, doing as they pleased. The idea was that there was no hurry, no rush. It was all about spending time together. Since Elizabeth's only real goal was to see St. Peter's Square and the Vatican Museum, they decided to make that their top priority. They walked out onto the street and it didn't take long before they found the perfect café. Since their attempts at learning Italian failed miserably, they counted on English speaking—or at least English-understanding—restaurant personnel. If not, they figured they would point at food and pray for the right outcome.

"May I offer you some water?" asked the gal in the restaurant. "With our without gas?"

Beth was startled by the odd question until Luke told her the question must mean did they want plain or carbonated water. Luke then winked at Beth and said, "We're off to a perfect start."

Two steps forward…

Chapter Sixteen

Christianity is an incarnational faith.
Christianity makes the bold claim that,
since God became a human being, the
nexus in all the universe where humanity
meets divinity is right here, right now, in
our mundane physical world.

~ Carl McColman

Miriam began her day with *The Amidah*, or what is called "The Standing Prayer." Miriam recalled the history of the Colosseum and knew that the history of *The Amidah* for her people was also a reminder of the past and a way to bring God's blessings into the present and also the future. It was established by Ezra and was part of *The Talmud.*

It is considered a conversation with God and should only be interrupted in a dire circumstance. Miriam loved the beauty of the symbolism and she reverently stood to pray the eighteen blessings. There in her hotel in Italy she turned and faced Israel and took three small steps forward—signaling that she was approaching the King. According to some *Amidah* scholars, this was just as Abraham approached God on behalf of the inhabitants of Sodom and Gomorrah.

With her feet together she humbly bowed and then quietly began with words only audible to herself and her Creator.

For the blessing of the God of history she prayed:

> *"Blessed are you, O Lord our Elohim and Elohim of*
> *our fathers, the Elohim of Abraham, the Elohim of*

Isaac, and the Elohim of Jacob, the great, mighty and revered El, the Most High Elohim who bestows lovingkindnesses, the creator of all things, who remembers the good deeds of the patriarchs and in love will bring a redeemer to their children's children for his name's sake. O king, helper, savior and shield. Blessed are you, O Lord, the shield of Abraham."

For the blessing of nature she prayed:

"You, O Lord, are mighty forever, you revive the dead, you have the power to save. You cause the wind to blow and the rain to fall. You sustain the living with lovingkindness, you revive the dead with great mercy, you support the falling, heal the sick, set free the bound and keep faith with those who sleep in the dust. Who is like you, O doer of mighty acts? Who resembles you, a king who puts to death and restores to life, and causes salvation to flourish? And you are certain to revive the dead. Blessed are you, O Lord, who revives the dead."

Miriam continued on praying for the sanctification of God and for understanding. When Miriam prayed for repentance and forgiveness, she struck her breast symbolizing the deep pain in her heart at having caused a separation between herself and God because of her sins and yet trusting in His mercy and kindness.

"Bring us back, O Father, to your instruction; Draw us near, O our King, to your service; And cause us to return to you in perfect repentance, Blessed are you, O Lord, who delights in repentance.

"Forgive us, O our Father, for we have sinned; Pardon us, O our King, for we have transgressed; for you

pardon and forgive. Blessed are you, O Lord, who is merciful and always ready to forgive."

The words settled into Miriam's spirit like a bulb planted in springtime and now taking root. She continued praying for deliverance from affliction, for healing, for deliverance from want, for the gathering of the exiles and for the righteous reign of God.

If possible the words prayed for the destruction of apostates and the enemies of God seemed to rise before her very eyes, dancing towards heaven; and Miriam knew Adonai was with her this very day.

"Let there be no hope for slanderers, and let all wickedness perish in an instant. May all your enemies quickly be cut down, and may you soon in our day uproot, crush, cast down and humble the dominion of arrogance. Blessed are you, O Lord, who smashes enemies and humbles the arrogant."

Quietly she continued, barely audible, but just as it should be; she prayed for the righteous and proselytes, for the rebuilding of Jerusalem, for the messianic king, for the answering of prayer, for the restoration of temple service and for thanksgiving for God's unfailing mercies. She concluded with the last blessing which was for peace:

"Grant peace, welfare, blessing, grace, benevolent kindness and mercy to us and to all Israel your people. Bless us, O our Father, one and all, with the light of your countenance; for by the light of your countenance you have given us, O Lord our El, a Torah of life, benevolent kindness and salvation, blessing, mercy, life and peace. May it please you to bless your people Israel at all times and in every hour with your peace. Blessed

are you, O Lord, who blesses his people Israel with peace."

After her prayers, Miriam showered, ate a quick breakfast of oatmeal and a cup of coffee in the hotel's cafeteria, and headed out towards St. Peter's Square. Elizabeth came to mind again and Miriam quickly added her American friend to her prayers. Once in the square, just in time for the papal audience, Miriam found herself feeling rather peaceful. Quite the opposite feeling she expected to be having; clearly the protection she had asked for in her morning prayers was hers. *Did that mean she would need it?* She didn't really want to entertain that question and let it be released into the air of St. Peter's Square with hopes that it, too, would be brought to heaven by the many praying souls who were already in the square anxiously awaiting the pope's appearance.

Miriam knew the pope to be a man of great intellect and a man committed to the truth of his faith. She thought about the story of Joseph's parents meeting one another and their different views on social justice and the caring for the needs of others and couldn't help but believe that this pope seemed to have bridged the gap between the two views. On the one hand, he preached and wrote about the ways in which mankind was called to respond to the needs of others; yet on the other hand he preached and wrote about freedom to respond to that call as each saw fit. However, the caveat was always the same: freedom didn't translate into an "anything goes" way of living; rather, freedom translated into the freedom to do what was true and right. He impressed Miriam. He impressed the peoples of many nations.

And that is what made his life a threat.

It was a threat to every person and group who wanted freedom to be the "anything goes" way of life—and if it weren't for this man and the others in the Four Horsemen contingency, maybe the "anything goes" way of life would be a foregone conclusion.

The irony didn't escape Miriam: how could people so adamant in their beliefs that everyone should be able to do anything, be the same people who did not allow people of faith to flourish? Instead, they became targets. Their livelihoods became precarious at best when they were labeled as hate-mongers and identified as bigots. People refused to do business with these people of faith and they eventually stood alone: no one to stand up for them. The thought of those same sorts of people of faith—and their horrendous deaths in the Colosseum—crept into Miriam's mind and heart. Her lips moved silently with prayer.

It was becoming a very volatile world situation with no end in sight. Miriam knew, firsthand, how long the situation had been under observation before the idea of a counter plan was entertained. Miriam was deep in thought when the crowd roared and the pope was driven in his small vehicle, around and through the square before taking his place on the platform.

†

Lunch was perfect. Luke had cannelloni and Elizabeth enjoyed a caprese salad. Each had a glass of wine and didn't feel any urgent need to get up from their places of comfort with its perfect view of passers-by. Eventually, however, Luke made the gallant gesture of getting them to their one purposeful destination and Beth complied. "Are you ready, honey? Is there anything else you would like?"

"No, I'm good. Go ahead and get the bill and we'll be on our way. I can see the throngs of people and the statues of the apostles from here! I am getting excited to go."

By the time Beth and Luke arrived at St. Peter's Square, they had already missed the pope's traversing of the area but did not feel slighted. It wasn't as if they would have been able to speak with him or receive his personal blessings. No, this was fine they both decided as they took their place in a back row made up of black plastic folding chairs.

Chapter Seventeen

This man has not yet seen his final hour,
although so close to it his folly brought
him that little time was left to change his
ways.

~ Dante

As was the custom at St. Peter's Square, Archbishops introduced different contingencies to the pope. At each announcement the square filled with applause emanating from the group whose introduction was being made. It didn't matter if the group had dozens of members or just a few people, the enthusiasm was the same. Out of respect and shared understanding at the prospect of being in the same proximity of the pope, the remaining audience dutifully clapped as well.

After all the introductions had been made—from religious sisters visiting from the Horn of Africa to a Boy Scout troop from the United States—the pope took his place.

The crowd roared.

Cameras flashed and videos were held high above the heads of all in hopes of catching something for posterity's sake.

The Swiss Guard, in all their colorful regalia, was at full alert.

As he began speaking, first in English, then Latin, then French, a silence rolled across the seats like a wave arriving on shore. At first it was just in the distance, and before Luke and Beth realized it, it had washed its way to their back row seats.

The audience was completely silent.

In front, Miriam kept her eyes darting from one location to another. The slightest movement brought her immediate attention. Every hair on her neck was standing at attention. She was prepared for anything; for everything. She listened as the pope spoke.

"Many people do not believe in God or His existence. They entertain such thoughts as: How can there be a God when such terrible things happen in the world? Where is God when a young mother dies from cancer and leaves a grieving husband and four small children? Why is God allowing corrupt and sadistic men to sell young girls for prostitution? How can God allow a priest to molest a young boy?

"These are all real and valid questions! I, too, ask questions. But I have come to see that the bigger question is: Where are believers in these tragedies? How are the followers of Christ helping those in need? Why aren't people loving one another as Jesus asked us to do?

"My brothers and sisters, it is time for us to make a decision. What path will we choose? It is time for each of us to see that it may be more sinful, more evil, to be a lukewarm believer than not to believe at all. Let us not forget that Christ has said that to whom much is given, much is expected. Was He telling us that as followers we will be more responsible than those who don't believe? Will we be responsible, as disciples, to affect the lives of non-believers in such a way as to become a catalyst for their belief?

"Yes, that is what our Savior was telling us; for He knew of this time in history when our culture would make

us forget that we serve a God who has asked us to be His arms and legs. He knew of this time in history when we would have before us life and death and would choose death—a slow death that arises from a lack of passion and truth.

"We cannot go on if we are divided amongst ourselves. Again, Jesus knew this and warned us. He's given us all we need. Now it is time to put on our armor and fight the good fight. We are being called to persecution in His name. Are we ready? Are you ready? Am I ready? Is the world ready for what is to come if we do not immediately become all that Jesus has asked us to become? Let us not forget that we have been warned that the Son of Man will return like a thief in the night—at a time unknown to us, a time unexpected.

"It is time to expect His return."

The pope's voice was quivering with emotion. Viewers who were watching from their home television sets were shaken with the words the pontiff was saying. Conviction was felt throughout the flock.

†

The questions hung in the air of St. Peter's Square. They hung in the living rooms of the thousands of homes who weekly watched the pope's address. They were questions that demanded answers.

†

Miriam knew her answer. Yes, she was ready. She prayed this morning and knew that her prayers were her armor. She remembered something Joseph had once said. If she recalled correctly, he said it was a quote from St. Ignatius—and it was something his mother always said to him: "Pray like it depends on God; work like it depends on you."

Miriam liked that; it reminded her of an old Jewish fable about a man who asked his rabbi if he should tie up his donkey at night or if he should trust God would take care of the donkey. The rabbi responded: "Trust God, but tie up the donkey."

This was exactly what the pontiff was now saying to his flock: know that God is here and act on his behalf.

†

Elizabeth held Luke's hand a bit more tightly than usual. The questions the pope asked swirled around in her mind. She thought about the death that struck unexpectedly while she was in the Holy Land. She thought about her own lukewarm attitude when she was with her friends and family. She didn't want to be deemed "crazy" or "radical" and kept her thoughts to herself when they talked about abortion or contraception. *Was she worse than a non-believer?* The thought made her feel ill.

†

The pontiff's questions—and his alarming warnings—continued to ricochet around the square. This was nothing like his previous addresses wherein he spoke words of hope and faith. The Boy Scouts gathered in the front row of St. Peter's were getting bored, clearly the excitement of the morning was now winding down and their young minds were already seeking the next great adventure. Cries were heard from some of the babies in the crowd. People began rustling in their chairs.

Since it was a sunny day with clear skies, the massive stone obelisk in the middle of St. Peter's Square was able to act as a sundial. Noon was upon the crowd.

Elizabeth felt a chill run up and down her spine despite the warm temperatures. She shivered.

"Are you alright?" Luke queried with a sideways glance in her direction.

"Yes," Beth offered without much conviction. She searched her mind for what was bothering her and then, for some odd reason, remembered that Catholics believed that the holiest time of the day was noon to three o'clock which represented the time their Savior— her Savior—was nailed to a cross until He gave up His last breath and offered himself to God.

†

Miriam stood to get a better look at the crowd when she heard a loud crack and a woman's scream. Miriam looked towards the stage and saw that the pontiff was being ushered off by the Swiss Guard. Taking no chances, they were surrounding him with their bodies and moving him to safe quarters. Other members of the Swiss Guard were running towards the area from which the popping sound had emanated. Still others were using their extended arms to guide the crowds towards the streets, emptying St. Peter's Square.

Chapter Eighteen

The hand of the Lord came upon me, and
he led me out in the spirit of the Lord and
set me in the center of the plain, which was
now filled with bones. He made me walk
among them in every direction so that I
saw how many they were on the surface of
the plain. How dry they were!

~ Ezekiel 37:1-2

Pandemonium broke out. Luke grabbed Elizabeth's hand and would not let go. No matter what lay ahead, he was not going to be separated from his wife. Together they ran towards the makeshift gates which had been, in all the commotion, knocked down. People were running and shouting. The Swiss guards were doing their best to keep everyone calm but the throngs of people would have nothing to do with it. A stampede ensued.

†

Protocol dictated that Miriam meet the others at the catacombs—the predetermined gathering site—for the rendezvous. She found Joseph, Abdul, and Joffa. Aayan, the Muslim cleric was safe as were the rabbis, Abdas and Abdul. The pope, too, was secure.

Miriam's breathing, while labored, was quickly under control. She perused the catacomb and took her spot by the other agents.

At different points in time over the past two years, everyone had been informed as to the mission that lay ahead. Without a hitch, and certainly through God's graces, all were of the same mind: serving God and making His holy will known was more important than ever. The world was in total chaos. Economies were collapsing and whole nations were at war. Civil unrest and disobedience existed within the borders of many countries.

It was time to make the world recognize the path of destruction that it had chosen and turn back from that path. That was the essence of the pope's message. It was not too late, as many doomsayers predicted. Surely mankind was on a dangerous precipice, but that would make God's intercession all the more glorious! That was the message of the Four Horsemen.

Speaking fluent English, the shared language of the entire gathering, the Muslim cleric said, "May we begin with a prayer?"

All agreed by nodding their heads. Clandestine meetings between the four men had happened on as many as three occasions that Miriam was aware of and in those meetings all four of the religious leaders had formed a bond that existed because of their faith, a faith that far exceeded anything Miriam had ever witnessed. It was the sort of faith she knew her parents had, as did her brother David; but what set the faith of these four men apart was that it existed in a setting where, if history was any indicator, enemies were within reach of each other. Jew, Christian, and Muslim sat side by side to discuss the fate of the world.

They were kind men, they were humble men.

Prayers were said with a certainty that God would prevail even in this dark and desperate time.

†

By some miracle, Elizabeth and Luke made it back to their apartment unscathed. The crowds attempting to leave St. Peter's Square were pushing in on them and yet they managed to hang on to each other. Heaving themselves into their apartment, they collapsed against the door and slid to the floor. Neither wanted to be the first to speak. Articulating the events of the morning would only make them authentic; and at this point, neither Beth nor Luke had any desire to delve into the reality of what had just happened.

After a few minutes, Luke managed to regain his composure—his sense of taking the bull by the horns, as it were—and resiliently stood as if the action itself had meaning.

"Are you okay? Is anything hurt? Do you feel alright?"

Beth wanted to reassure him and offer some sort of response that would allow both of them to move from the door to the couch where they might better discuss what they had just experienced. She reached her hand out to Luke who took it and helped her to her feet as she said, "Yes, honey. I'm a little shaken but I'm fine. No apparent injuries. No obvious cuts or bruises. Now what?"

Luke looked around the room. He saw, for the first time, the picture of Jesus hanging on the wall. If he was not mistaken, it was called the "Sacred Heart" and he knew that Beth had one in the library of their home. He had never really been sure what to make of it—with its picture of Jesus with open hands, semi-outstretched arms and a heart visible on his chest; a heart with flames erupting from the top and a cross in the midst of the flames. But now, he somehow found the picture comforting.

Luke also quickly realized the significance of having no television set in the apartment. Something major had just happened in St. Peter's Square and he—they—had no way to find out what it was!

Luke's eyes then settled on the rosary that sat on the table next to the couch. It seemed inviting. Luke wasn't often prone to praying the rosary but felt it was perfect for him and Beth to do just that right now.

"How about joining me for a rosary?" Luke gently—and uncharacteristically—asked Beth.

Her response was to walk over to the rosary, pick it up in her hands, kiss the Cross and kneel on the floor.

Luke joined her and they began.

†

Behind them stood Archangel Michael. Unseen by their eyes, he was clad in soldier's gear: silver-plated armor covered his chest and leather strappings covered his arms and legs. He held a large sword in his right hand that would seem to most to be unwieldy—except for Michael's mammoth size—while he held a shield in his left hand. St. Michael bowed his head and silently prayed with Luke and Beth. He knew it would be the prayers of the faithful that would move the hands of heaven in the war that lie ahead.

After the rosary, Beth found herself suggesting the prayer of St. Michael. Luke did not know the prayer but kept his head low and eyes shut as his wife recited it, apparently from heart:

> *Saint Michael the Archangel, defend us in battle. Be our protection against the wickedness and snares of the devil.*

May God rebuke him, we humbly pray; and do Thou, O Prince of the Heavenly Host - by the Divine Power of God - cast into hell, satan and all the evil spirits, who roam throughout the world seeking the ruin of souls. Amen.

Chapter Nineteen

All the contemplative life asks of us is that
we be willing to move forward in faith, one
step at a time.

~ Carl McColman

When the prayers had finished, Joseph looked around the catacomb and made the decision to begin with what appeared to be the only facts they knew, "The pope may have just been the target of an assassin attempt. Initial reports have not yet been made but we have to assume the worst case scenario. We have to assume that the groups who have obtained the intel about this mission know that these four men are gathered here and intend to deliver their messages as planned. Today's attack—we would be remiss if we assumed it was anything other than an attempt on the pope's life—confirms that we are compromised."

All agreed.

Joseph continued, and his head nodded in the direction of each of the leaders as he spoke their code names, "It is my understanding that each of you have made the commitment to see this through—even at great personal cost. I understand and agree. The agents gathered here also freely offer their lives for this cause.

"We've seen the collapse of economies throughout the world, attacks on all places of worship—regardless of faith—and we've witnessed as the disintegration of the family has happened at breakneck speed.

"Keeping all this in mind, and knowing the failure of such organizations as the United Nations, and attempts at a world currency, the leaders gathered together under the Four Horsemen project are all willing to suffer for their decision to stop the destruction of humankind as created by the almighty God."

Chapter Twenty

The spirit of the Lord shall rest upon him:
a spirit of wisdom and of understanding,
A spirit of counsel and of strength, a spirit
of knowledge and of fear of the Lord.

~ Isaiah 11:2-3

Miriam spoke first. She didn't know how she knew what she did, but she knew it nonetheless. She wasn't sure if she could find the right words so she asked for a bit of heavenly guidance and then authoritatively said, "Today's attempt on the life of White Dove was meant to derail this important mission. Its failure was due to a heavenly hand in a way in which no one was harmed— very much like the hand of Mary who deflected the bullet intended for John Paul's assassination many years ago. The veil between heaven and earth is being pulled back and we are being asked to step into the gap—to become the intercessors who work on behalf of believers around the world. This mission will require sacrifice and wisdom; it will bring us to our knees in prayer but will raise us up in hope and joy. We will see the fruits of our obedience and will be partakers of the peace and harmony that will one day envelop the whole world."

All the men in the room simply stared at her. In the back of Joseph's mind he could hear his mother telling him about gifts and charisms. He tried to wrestle them to his consciousness and pluck out her teachings on what she called "words of knowledge" or prophecy. He failed but somehow knew that what Miriam spoke was based upon some gift she was given by God for this specific situation. Since he couldn't put it into words—

and wasn't exactly sure what it was he was grappling with—he remained quiet.

The silence in the catacomb was deafening. Miriam was sure the others could hear her heart hammering violently in her chest. Adrenaline was coursing through her veins and her temples were pounding. Her entire body was on full alert and she felt as if she had super-powers like some silly cartoon character, so much so was her body electrified by the past few minutes.

Finally, Joffa spoke. The rabbis that were under his protection moved in unison, their bodies turning slightly to the left so as to face him more completely.

"If we believe in our mission, if we have faith in our Creator, we must see this event as coming from the hand of God—our God, the one who binds us all together. We cannot say one thing to the world and live an entirely different way. Do we believe that our God is all-powerful and capable of anything?"

All men nodded in agreement with Aayan, the Muslim cleric, falling prostrate on the ground and offering praise to God. The others followed in quick pursuit; each choosing a physical posture that best represented his or her deepest held conviction that God was, indeed, all-powerful; and that He was choosing this place and time to enter the world to offer hope one last time.

At first the voices were only whispers, spoken in each person's native language; but soon there was a rhythm—a joining of different tongues into one and a melding of words into a cohesive prayer.

Miriam recognized the psalm of David they all now prayed under the guidance of God, blessed be His holy name:

Have mercy on me, God,

>*For I am treated harshly;*

>*Attackers press me all the day.*

My foes treat me harshly all the day;

>*Yes, many are my attackers.*

O Most High, when I am afraid,

>*In you I place my trust.*

God, I praise your promise;

>*In you I trust, I do not fear.*

>*What can mere flesh do to me?*

All the day they foil my plans;

>*Their every thought is of evil against me.*

They hide together in ambush;

>*They watch my every step;*

>*They lie in wait for my life.*

They are evil; watch them, God!

>*Cast down the nations in your anger!*

My wanderings you have noted;

>*Are my tears not stored in your vial,*

>*Recorded in your book?*

My foes turn back when I call on you,

>*This I know: God is on my side.*

God, I praise your promise;

In you I trust, I do not fear.

What can mere mortals do to me?

I have made vows to you, God;

With offerings I will fulfill them,

Once you have snatched me from death,

Kept my feet from stumbling,

That I may walk before God

In the light of the living.

After a few minutes, a soft breeze flowed through the room. At first it circled the floor and caught everyone quite off-guard since never before, in any of their gatherings, had they noticed such a draft nor could they imagine from where it came. Rising from their different positions, each now slowly stood as if the breeze had lifted them up. Miriam was reminded of the ballet in which she sat mesmerized by the gentle movements of the dancers on stage; now she was one of those dancers, being lifted by the spirit of God.

Within seconds, the breeze became stronger and continued to rise, higher and higher around their bodies and in the room. Miriam could feel it at her ankles then her shins and her knees. Invisible yet recognized, acknowledged. She looked across the room and saw that Joseph's shirt tails were now moving, taking on a life of their own as they swayed in the current. The candles remained lit in spite of the force that was now overtaking the room. The wind was getting noticeably stronger and soon Miriam's hair was being blown around her face; dust from the floor was filling the room as if there were a small tornado in their midst. It was no longer easy to breathe. The rabbis attempted to wipe their eyes as the dust became thicker and seeing became more difficult.

But no one was afraid; fear had not penetrated the occupants of the room. Rather, they opened their arms in acceptance. Knowing became theirs. Wisdom was at their side. Courage and conviction penetrated each person, taking up residence in the hearts and souls of all who had gathered.

Miriam knew her ancestors stood with her; she knew that by her side was Sarah, the first matriarch, and Rebecca, mother-in-law to Rachel and Leah. Miriam reflected on her teachings about Judge Deborah the strong and vibrant woman; a woman on fire for her faith whose advocacy towards justice was a component of what originally inspired Miriam to join Mossad. Miriam never tired of hearing how Judge Deborah sat under a palm tree and heard the stories of her people, of God's people—and made decisions, cast verdicts, settled disputes. Judge Deborah was honored and respected. As a young girl Miriam went to sleep at night drawn into the story and becoming one of the characters. She reenacted the account of Deborah and Barak as they entered battle against the oppressive rule of Jabin, king of Canaan. In her reenactment, Miriam was Judge Deborah. Miriam was the warrior, the prophetess. It wasn't Miriam's ego that put her in those roles but her unquenchable desire to serve God—to do His bidding, to serve His people.

Ayala would be proud to think that all the stories she told a young Miriam about Judge Deborah had not only emboldened Miriam in her heart's desire, but certainly set the path upon which she currently treads. Now, Miriam prayed, that Ayala had been written in the

Book of Life and that Miriam would one day join her in her eternal reward.

As the dust settled and the winds crept from the room as mysteriously as they had arrived, Miriam couldn't help but wonder, *Is Moshiach now returning? Is this the time when the Messiah gathers us all from the corners of the earth and paradise reigns?*

Chapter Twenty-One

*We made our way along that lonely plain
like men who seek the right path they have
lost, counting each step a loss till it is
found.*

~ Dante

Joseph watched as Miriam stood motionless in the room. He felt, rather than saw, the winds recede. It was time to move forward and so he said, "I believe we all know what we have to do now. It seems to me that the spirit of God has confirmed for us what Miriam prophetically spoke just moments ago: that our mission remains the same. This visit from the spirit of God was meant to give us wisdom and hope."

Joseph looked around the room to see if, indeed, all agreed with his statements thus far. All eyes were upon him and indicated a clear belief that the time to coalesce was now. If God were testing those gathered in this room, the testing would prove them all ready and willing to move ahead. The testing would prove them all to be soldiers for the battle that would inevitably change the world.

Joseph then continued, "Christian Scripture states that we do not fight a battle against flesh and blood but against powers unseen. It says we fight against principalities that are dark and wicked. But what we have come to learn is that those powers have taken on human form; they have brought the spiritual battle to the earthly realm and we are now required to fight it on two fronts.

"It is appropriate that this mission is, on the one hand, made up of those whose highest call is to serve God: White Dove, Aayan, Abdas and Abdeel; while on the other hand it is made up of those whose highest call is to serve country: myself, Miriam, Abdul, and Joffa. I believe that together, we will be able to combat—and win—the spiritual forces that have now taken human form."

Joffa posed the first, most important question: "Do we know who these people are?"

"We do," Joseph confirmed. "If we don't know them by name we know them by their fruits. Right now we see them as well-placed statesmen in each of our respective countries. They are working tirelessly to undermine all the laws of God and replace them with the laws of man. They have relied on a mole—an informant—within our own ranks to accomplish their work.

"Clearly this has allowed them the first strike against us: to make an attempt on the life of White Dove and remove the threat of the Four Horsemen against their agenda. This strike, even though it failed, will help them accomplish—or believe they will accomplish—what we know to be one of their highest, most insidious desires: to introduce and assure passage of various man-made laws that will continue to undermine the laws of God. They are tasked with destroying home and family and replacing those foundations of society with ill-conceived notions using the same titles. Moral decay is at the root of their plan. It is a good plan because countries filled with despair and collapse create a vacuum in which evil will fill—and thrive. These well-placed statesmen are loved by their countrymen and are seen as "progressive" and "open-minded" but their agendas will neither take our countries forward nor will they create the utopian existence that is touted as their consequence. They are already well on the road to success which makes our mission all the more difficult. It will be near-impossible to turn back the hands of time; but turn them back we must. It is only through repentance and knowledge of truth that we will be able to rebuild our nations, our world."

†

After completing their prayers, Elizabeth's first response was to call the children. "Please, Luke, see if you can get the kids on the phone. I need to know they are okay; that they are safe. I can only imagine what is going through their minds if they have watched any of this on television."

Luke dutifully took out his cell phone and first called Sophia. He knew that while Beth was concerned for all her children equally, her daughter would be in the foremost part of her mind. Even though Sophia was getting married, Luke knew that she would always be his baby girl as well. "Hi sweetie!" Luke cheerfully said into the phone. In those few seconds that it took to push speed dial his head filled with the most unimaginable things that could be happening back home. So when Sophia picked up right after the first ring, Luke's cheerfulness at hearing her voice was sincere.

"Hey dad! How are you? Are you guys okay?"

"Yes; but why do you ask?"

"Well, you just landed in Rome a few hours ago and I imagined you and mom would have completely forgotten about us by now—that's all. It just seems odd that you would call right away. No biggie."

Luke could hear the frustration in Sophia's voice and quickly put a band-aid on what could easily become a gaping wound: "Don't mind me. I'm tired from the flight. We just want to let you know we've landed safe and sound and check in before we forget about you the rest of the week!"

Sophia laughed and the tension eased a bit. "Sounds like a good plan. I'm with the boys right now and we are just getting ready to bar-b-que some chicken kabobs. Do you want to say 'hello' to them? Jeremy is on his way over, too."

Luke was glad to hear that Sophia's fiancé was on his way to their home. Luke genuinely liked his future son-in-law and knew that Sophia would be happy in their marriage. They were just about at the end of their pre-Cana wedding classes and the excitement of the upcoming nuptials was now part of their everyday lives. "Sure! Put them on speaker phone and I'll do the same with your mom."

Sophia called to her brothers and Luke motioned to Beth. With everyone on speaker phone at their respective ends, Beth gave them a quick update on the plane trip and confirmed that they all knew where she and Luke were staying. Elizabeth conveniently left out the glaring fact that there seemed to have been a major upheaval in Rome—especially since she had no facts and couldn't come up with one good reason to worry anyone. The call ended with everyone sharing their love and promises from the kids to eat well, drive carefully, and stay safe.

Only Luke and Beth knew the depths of their requests upon their kids.

Chapter Twenty-Two

Before I formed you in the womb I knew you.

~Jeremiah 1:5

Miriam had a difficult time falling asleep. She thought about the day's events and the words she was "inspired" to speak in the catacombs. She felt silly and yet knew that there was not a shred of ego involved in what she said. In some ways she didn't even want the words to be true. She wanted all this to end and to be back home with her father and brother enjoying a cup of coffee on the balcony. She wanted to be walking through the marketplace with her friends or sitting in her living room reading a good book.

That afternoon held no new information and, at Joseph's suggestion, everyone returned to their respective hotels. They were proceeding as had been previously planned but with a new, deeper understanding of what it meant to serve God and country.

The Vatican denied any rumors surrounding the incident at St. Peter's. Rather, they immediately released a press report that stated His Holiness had suddenly come down with the flu and was being tended to by his physician. Prayer requests were made and very quickly what had been complete pandemonium and chaos returned to normal. The pope was now resting comfortably in his Vatican apartment guarded and secure.

Miriam was struck by how easily people wanted to look the other way; how easily they would believe what was told to them so as to not have to seek, search, or find truths on their own. This is what made her job easier but is also what made people more vulnerable.

The Internet only added to people's misinformation and gullibility. If ever there was a time for the Messiah to return, this seemed to be it. *How much more moral decay, personal degradation, and self-centeredness could the world take before it would simply implode?* Miriam wondered to herself.

It often seemed so precarious at times that Miriam had difficulties not succumbing to her feelings of gloom and doom. But today, recalling how the spirit of God had washed over them in the catacombs, Miriam knew that God's hand was upon the world; she knew that He would not let them down even if she couldn't quite explain what that knowledge meant.

The Four Horseman mission was to bring the world to repentance and redemption but Miriam couldn't help but speculate if that was really in everyone's best interest. *Wouldn't the Messiah's return be a better solution?*

Finally, after hours of restlessness, she felt the spirit of God come over her just as surely as it had come across the waters during creation and she fell into a deep sleep.

†

Joseph's attempt to sleep was no different than Miriam's. He just did his tossing and turning, so to speak, on the streets of Rome. After departing from the group, Joseph walked aimlessly, trying to bring his chaotic thoughts under control. He deliberated the failed attempt on the pope's life and the quick Vatican cover-up. Quite frankly, Joseph agreed with how the

Vatican handled the situation. He would have done the same. It was prudent and would certainly help keep the damage at a minimum. And it left the Four Horsemen mission in a much better position as the culprits of the Vatican event would surely have expected the news to have spread like wildfire—and instead what they got was a no more impactful than a match lit in the rain.

Joseph also tried to evaluate his feelings about Miriam being involved in what was officially a dangerous mission. It was one thing to plan and to anticipate; but it was now quite another to have had the episode this afternoon. While it would be classified as "failed" in his report to his superiors, the fact that such a potential threat was able to make its way into St. Peter's Square at all still had merit. And that was the part that had Joseph worried about Miriam. Clearly his personal feelings were overpowering his professional ones.

Personally, he wanted to protect her. Ideally, he wanted her back in Israel in her father's apartment. Joseph wasn't sure if Miriam would appreciate his need to shield her from harm but it would be ridiculous to ignore his feelings.

Professionally, Joseph was amazed at Miriam's acumen in the situation. He knew she was a valuable asset for the task at hand and found himself looking to her for insight and guidance. Today proved that this inclination of his to seek her counsel was right-placed. She spoke with the wisdom of a sage and the tenacity of a focused, thoughtful agent.

In retrospect, it seemed to Joseph that Miriam was very much following God's lead in her life. Joseph admired her resolve and saw that her enthusiasm and conviction were contagious. He knew she began and ended her day with prayer and it suddenly occurred to

Joseph that this was the reason behind Miriam's ability to withstand whatever life brought: Miriam was always walking with God.

So it was that Joseph's last thought before falling into a restless, interrupted few hours of sleep happened to be the one question that now seemed most pressing, most important: *What does God want of me?*

†

Abdul plopped down on the floor at the foot of the bed as was his habit when on a mission. Experience had taught him to never, ever, be caught in bed, sound asleep when lives depended upon him. He had long trained himself to survive on cat-naps—those 20 minutes of sleep in which REM was achieved and yet the groggy, deep sleep that surround it was avoided. It kept him alert and yet rested.

The door to the adjoining room was left ajar so that both Abdul's ears and eyes were privy to whatever was happening in that space. At that particular moment in time the Muslim Cleric—Aayan—was in a deep sleep. His light snoring provided an oddly soothing backdrop to Abdul's own swatches of rest.

Abdul turned the events of the day over and over in his head. He trusted Joseph's experience and professionalism and yet nothing had prepared Abdul for what had taken place in the catacombs. He briefly thought of the winds and then the ensuing prayers in which all were in sync with one another. Abdul wasn't quite prepared for Miriam's words which sounded, to the untrained ear, very much like a script or a play. She spoke words that made sense and yet there seemed to be an authority about them that Abdul had never heard before. Her words were spoken with such clarity, with such command, that all who heard them knew them to be true. In particular Abdul liked when she spoke of being lifted up in joy and hope and the fruits of obedience.

Next, Abdul's mind replayed the wind that made its presence known in a firm but gentle way. Abdul was reminded of the way in which his mother would reprimand him. She was always firm but gentle; beneath anything she said or did was her unending love for her son and her genuine desire that he should grow into the man that God intended him to be. He smiled in the shadows of the night that now occupied the room as he thought of his mother and the wonderful times he had known in his home despite the poverty and lack that existed in their everyday lives. It was this feeling of belonging and of love that Abdul wished—prayed—that the world would know. His own life proved that neither possessions nor position were guarantees for a fulfilling life. In fact, Abdul could name more than a few friends and acquaintances that he had met along the way whose lives had actually been made worse by their wealth or their careers. Although younger than most of his friends, it didn't take too much time before Abdul recognized the great gift his loving mother had bestowed upon him—and the great call she demanded he answer: to live by God's laws all the days of his life.

†

Since Joffa's edict was to protect both Abdas and Abdeel—the Jewish rabbis—it became clear very quickly that the two men would need to share a room with their protector. To the best of his ability, Joffa honored their rituals and their traditions. As they chanted their evening prayers, Joffa remained silent and still. He did not want to introduce any distraction in the room and patiently waited until they had finished before he asked if it would be okay to use the shower.

Once done, Joffa set up a cot in the corner of the room and watched as the two men pulled a screen between the two large beds that took up most of the space. Each man interested in upholding the honor and dignity of the other.

It was only a few minutes before all three slid into a sound, deep sleep.

†

Luke held Beth in bed for a long time before either succumbed to the exhaustion of the day. By the time they mustered enough strength to leave the apartment and find a light dinner, they were less than hungry. More than anything else they needed to leave the apartment to feel that things were going to be all right. Inside it they felt trapped—as if the outside world held something evil and foreboding from which they needed to hide. They wanted to be on the streets with other tourists and natives simply enjoying the sights and sounds of Rome traffic and architecture. It was important that they not let the day's events get hold of them. Beth kept hearing over and over in her spirit words from Scripture: *Do not be afraid.*

While their excursion worked and provided the much-needed distraction, lying in bed brought them immediately back to the bizarre experience at St. Peter's Square that afternoon. Even the diversion of the evening walk and meal couldn't remove the questions from their minds.

Finally, after agreeing that it would do no one any good to stay up all night, they held tight onto one another and slipped into a surprisingly restful sleep while in the corner of the room Archangel Michael stood guard.

Chapter Twenty-Three

*One day, all human accomplishments will
be reduced to a pile of ashes. But every
single child to whom a woman has given
birth will live forever, for he has been given
an immortal soul made to God's image
and likeness.*

~ Alice von Hildebrand

The vote on the bill wasn't even close. No one expected it to be and yet there was always hope. People of faith prayed novenas, started prayer chains, and stormed the gates of Heaven for the intercession of angels and saints. The belief that the country could be turned back from the path of death and decay was palpable in every congregation around the country. God was much bigger than the black pall that had covered the nation. But male and female United States senators alike cast votes for unlimited access to government-funded abortion in every institution across the land. Every Catholic hospital, every secular place of business, every entrepreneur wanting to take a chance on the "American dream" would be taxed to collect the fees for the new Abortion Rights Tax Act. Religious freedom and rights of objection would no longer exist. Anyone refusing to pay the taxes would be closed down. All previous legal oppositions and lawsuits had been squelched, overturned, and exhausted. It was a time unlike any other in the short history of the United States of America.

The federal government would essentially be given free rein to board up and render useless any organization—no matter how big or how small—that did not immediately comply with the new law. A nation that once provided safe harbor for refugees fleeing from distant lands was no longer safe for the unborn. Women claimed complete control over their bodies—to use and be used as instruments of pleasure and objectification—and the government offered that control free of charge at any time during pregnancy. The nation completely capitulated to the culture of death that John Paul II had, only a few short years before, so aptly labeled.

†

All the United States senators were present. It was a mid-term election year and none could risk being absent from this important vote. It would either turn the country on its heels in one breathtaking move or it would be rocket fuel and provide such a catalyst for the road it was already going down that there would be no turning back.

It was time for repentance and a return to God but only two senators seemed to be speaking out against the atrocities that would soon become the fabric of the American way of life. They stood on the senate steps and proclaimed the evils of abortion; they withstood ridicule as they warned of the catastrophes that would befall the great nation should the Abortion Rights Tax Act be passed. News stations far and wide gave them coverage; but it was the sort of coverage that portrayed these two lone voices as radicals and not worth an intelligent, progressive, "thinking" man's time.

Watching the television screen in her apartment, Sophia and her friends waited as the pretty brunette news anchor prepared the viewers for the upcoming vote, "In a moment we will go live to the senate floor." Here she turned and with the microphone in her right hand, used her left to point out the building just beyond her left shoulder. While keeping her in the lower corner of the screen, the camera was able to capture the somber look on the faces of the senators as they walked past the two isolated men standing on the steps sounding more than a bit like John the Baptist. *All they needs is a hair suit and some locusts and they'll be all set*, Sophia thought wryly.

The men were senators themselves and must have hoped that their last minute pleas for reason and life would not fall on deaf ears.

"Let us not forget that this nation was founded on the great principles of a loving and merciful God!" the older senator with a well-lined face boomed.

"But His mercy will not last forever!" the other senator, younger and much taller, added.

One of the women senators who were filing past the two outcasts taunted loud enough for the camera to pick up, "Where is his mercy for women? Why should women bear the burden of unwanted and unplanned pregnancies?"

To that, the state legislators who were on their way to vote and thus still within ear shot nodded and a few made clapping motions with their hands. "Bravo!" they seemed to be saying to the women who questioned God's mercy towards women.

Sophia's friend Julie mimicked them and clapped her hands while mocking the disheveled appearance of the two men who were standing on the steps. "Seriously, Soph! If they wanted to be taken seriously they at least needed to iron their shirts. I mean, come on! What's with the whole doom-and-gloom prophet look?"

Sophia was in the process of formulating a response that would honor the wisdom that her mother had so painstakingly tried to impart over the past few years while also placating her friend's sincere belief that women ought to be able to have as much sexual freedom as their male counterparts without having to deal with consequences. Guilt washed over Sophia at the way in which she had treated her mom when all her mom was really trying to do was enlighten Sophia to what Beth often called the "objective truths." Beth must have been making headway because as Sophia listened to the mocking female senators on their way to vote for the indiscriminate abortion bill, Sophia could feel herself wanting to tell these women that they misunderstood mercy and that more than anyone could imagine, God loved women and was on their side*! Isn't that what Jesus came to show? He was a radical feminist—and in a good way!* Sophia had to congratulate her mom as these thoughts surfaced in her own heart and mind.

Sophia didn't answer but Julie didn't seem to notice. They were all watching intently as the attractive brunette, whose name was apparently "Amber Matthews" according to the text banner at the bottom of the screen, juggled the microphone and positioned herself to take up the full screen. The banner also proclaimed that Amber was "reporting live." Clearly Amber was new to this sort of live reporting because she looked like she really wanted to turn the camera off and reposition herself and touch up her hair which was being blown about in the wind.

Matthews quickly chimed in for her followers who were, Sophia was guessing, more interested in the two disheveled men than they were willing to admit, "Well, Jason, it looks like the two senators from Alabama are alone in their views. In fact, it seems fair to say that these men may be the only two who do not recognize the need for the wonderful new bill to be enacted so that, *finally*, women will be equal to men!" The reporter had practically spit out the word "finally" as if women had more need for the abortion bill than they did for good healthcare or decent employment. *This is ridiculous!* Sophia found herself thinking.

Sophia's other friend, Meghan, jumped out of her seat and applauded. Both Sophia and Julie were taken by surprise at Meghan's response since neither knew about Meghan's abortion. Most recently, they had witnessed their once-exuberant friend go from joy to melancholy. Where once she seemed passionate and excited about everything, now Meghan seemed without a real enthusiasm for anything. They had grown to love her—and each other—deeply over the years of their friendship and now Sophia and Julie had often found themselves wanting to protect Meghan—against what, they just weren't sure—as she seemed always only half engaged in the world around her. "A shadow of her former self" would have aptly applied to describing Meghan.

"Wow, Meghan! We sure didn't see that coming," was all Julie could say. Sophia remained silent, taking it all in. If there's anything she'd learned from her mother, it was that nothing was ever as it seemed. She remembered her mother's trip to Israel a few years ago and how Sophia and her brothers all learned that the marriage of their parents wasn't a bed of roses—except maybe for the thorns. Although Sophia didn't think they would have actually divorced, she knew it was a difficult and sad time for both her mom and dad. This trip to Rome was the result of the effort they had put into their marriage and proof that things could be turned around. *If only our nation could experience the same sort of repentance,* Sophia found herself thinking and wondered when her mother's ideologies had become her own.

"I know," Meghan admitted. "It's just that people really don't have any idea what it is like for a girl to be pregnant and have no one to turn to and not be able to imagine the future."

With that, both Sophia and Julie looked at each other and then back to Meghan. Sophia gently asked, "Meghan, is there something you would like to tell us? Is there something you need us to know?"

Meghan turned to face the window but her friends could see her shoulders lightly moving up and down. Sophia got up from her seat on the couch and walked over to where Meghan now sat, quietly sobbing. Sophia and Meghan spent a few minutes staring out the window at the beautiful sky filled with cumulus clouds which were taking on all sorts of shapes and sizes. One of them reminded Sophia of a stuffed animal she had treasured as a young child. It was a rabbit who had seen far too many washings and had lost all its shape and yet the more worn it got, the more Sophia cherished it. It tugged at her heart and she had made her mom promise to feed Joy (her name for her rabbit) and play with her during the day while Sophia was at school. When Sophia would return home, the first thing she looked for upon entering the front door was Joy. Beth never failed to have the rabbit sitting on the coach welcoming Sophia home. Sophia watched as the Joy-shaped cloud slid out of view and wondered whatever had ever become of the real Joy.

After a few minutes, Sophia turned her gaze from the window towards her friend. Sophia saw the tears rolling off Meghan's face and onto her lap where her folded hands sat. The short, quick movements of Meghan's shoulders continued to reflect the deep pain that was erupting from the depths of her heart and soul.

Sophia pointed to the Kleenex box which was on the end table closest to Julie and Julie quietly picked it up and pulled a tissue from it and handed both the tissue and box to Sophia. Julie then knelt down on the floor by Meghan's feet while Sophia dabbed at the tears still running down Meghan's face. They sat like this for some time, the three friends, each desperately lost in her own world and yet realizing that their worlds were not separate but were one.

No one sought to break into the stillness that enveloped them because although they were silent, the love was palpable. It was obvious. They could all feel it and they wanted it to last forever—to define who they were as friends and as people. It was an amazing moment suspended in time. Sophia knew it was, as her mother would say, a "consolation." It was God pulling the veil back and putting His hand upon them.

As the silence continued, Sophia fondly recalled the first time they met in high school. Meghan, the effervescent, bubbly freshman asking to sit at the lunch table where Sophia and Julie sat in silence brought each out of her shell in a way that none could have imagined. They quickly bonded and became the closest of friends.

That was why Meghan's change from that vibrant high school freshman to the withdrawn college junior had been so difficult for Sophia and Julie to understand. But they never walked away from their friend—and now they were about to find out what had happened to the Meghan that they had met in high school; a young girl who continued to be a reminder of what love and kindness could do in any given situation.

"Remember Brian?" Meghan began.

"Sure!" Julie eagerly responded to Meghan's question. "Yeah. I remember he was really gorgeous and seemed actually quite nice. He wasn't as full of himself as some of the other guys we've met at school."

"Why?" was all Sophia wanted to know. Sophia agreed with Julie but knew that Brian's good looks and decent demeanor wasn't what this was going to be about. Her stomach lurched in anticipation of what she imagined was coming next.

"Well, he was nice. And he was cute. And he was a lot of fun. I got along great with his sister even though she was still in high school. She would come up with his parents on weekends every once in a while and take Brian and me to breakfast. It was really very nice." Quietly Meghan added, "I loved it."

Sophia had always admired Meghan since Meghan's parents had been divorced and Meghan wasn't always welcome in either of the new households that they had created. Her dad went on to get married and had a few kids and her mom did the same. Meghan sort of split her time between here, there, and everywhere. It seemed like a difficult situation at best but Meghan didn't dwell on it too much. When the going got tough, Meghan found escape with her friends. They'd go shopping, have sleepovers and gossip about snotty girls at school, and dream about boys. They imagined futures with big homes and fancy cars. They were pretty sure they'd each have the perfect kids and for Julie that meant a boy and two girls—in that order. Meghan, on the other hand, wanted what she called a "passel" of kids. She didn't care how many or what combinations. For Sophia's part, she always thought about how much she loved her brothers and since she had no sisters could only imagine a house with sons; maybe part of that dream was she didn't want a daughter who caused her grief the way she had done to her own mother.

All in all, their gossiping and dreaming was all rather harmless and it always stayed within their close group. Nonetheless, Sophia knew that deep in Meghan's heart lived a dream of belonging. That was why she wanted to surround herself with tons of children. She was going to create the home she never had. Now, Meghan just wanted to fit in with a family—any family it sometimes seemed. And as Sophia listened to Meghan talk about Brian's family, Sophia knew that this family had provided Meghan what she had secretly longed for her whole life: a place where she belonged.

"I loved those times. They were different from when we all hang out because I was welcomed into Brian's family in a different way. It just felt great. And peaceful. Actually, I'm not sure I can exactly explain it but I loved it. I belonged there and that made all the other parts of my life right. I hope you aren't offended by what I'm saying. I know that I 'belong' with you two and your families are always very loving to me; but with a boy it's different: you can see a future, I guess.

"So when Brian wanted to have a physical relationship, it made sense to me. It was the last piece of the puzzle in our relationship and it fit perfectly. And I loved him. I loved his family and could feel their love for me."

Sophia hugged Meghan to give her courage to continue and Julie, still sitting on the floor at Meghan's feet, patted Meghan's knee with her hand. Julie then clasped her hands over Meghan's hands which still sat in her lap as she had not moved an inch since she began talking.

Meghan then continued, "Of course, when I became pregnant I was stunned. I'm not sure why I should have been—that is just my luck—but there I was: pregnant. I told Brian. I played out the scenario many times beforehand and in each instance, the response I envisioned was completely different than what I actually got. I simply didn't picture his reaction—and would not have in a million years. I guess that's what I get for being a dreamer!"

Sophia quickly but firmly chimed in, "God created in you an enormous sensitivity to life that allows you to dream big. Don't deny who you are and don't try to be different. Whatever you do, don't lose sight of who you are because of a boy!"

Meghan smiled at Sophia and went on. Her friends knew her very well and she found great comfort in that right now.

"He wanted me to get an abortion. He said we had our whole futures ahead of us and when he talked like that I could tell he didn't see our futures as being together. He didn't see them the way I do—did. For him, there was now—this time that we were having fun and all—and then there would be a future. A future that didn't include me.

"I was crushed."

Those last words Meghan said were barely audible; but their weight also crushed Sophia and Julie. While it was no time for recriminations, Sophia wanted to know and so had to ask: "Why didn't you tell us?"

"And then what?" was all Meghan said.

Julie, with her practical side now in charge, didn't want to force Meghan to revisit her decision. Rather, Julie said, "Meghan, sweetie, no matter what has happened, we are here for you now. If we could wipe out your pain and your sorrow, we would."

To that Sophia added, "Meghan, please don't continue to go through this alone. I know this was a huge step you just took to let us in on your hurt; but please, I beg you, don't close up now. You've said it out loud and that is the first step towards healing."

Elizabeth had worked as a volunteer at a pregnancy center when Sophia was in high school so Sophia knew that her mother would be able to help Meghan—as soon as her mother returned from Rome. In the meantime, they needed to keep their friend covered in love and prayers. This Sophia knew in the depths of her heart: God would not let their precious friend slip any further into her shell now that she had freely offered this information. Sophia felt silly but had to say it out loud to make it real.

"Meghan, God loves you. You are his beloved daughter and your pain is His pain. This is why He sent his Son: so that you don't have to carry this burden alone. I remember when my mom worked at the center a few years ago and she said that one of the greatest gifts we have—and very rarely accept—is Jesus' forgiveness. Maybe because we don't do a very good job at forgiving ourselves so we figure how can this guy, who we don't really see, forgive us? But think about it— imagine the cross He carried. It was real. He didn't do it for himself. He did it for me! And for you! And for Julie!"

Julie started to cry. These were words she hadn't heard much but they certainly weren't new. And yet somehow when Sophia was saying them just now, they touched Julie's heart. Maybe because Julie knew that Jesus loved Meghan and recognized that she wasn't any different from Meghan in Jesus' eyes. The tears were streaming down her face when they all heard the boom of one of the men on the senate steps say, "Behold the dwelling of God is with men. He will dwell with them, and they shall be His people, and God Himself will be with them; He will wipe away every tear from their eyes, and death shall be no more, neither shall there be mourning nor crying nor pain any more, for the former things have passed away. It is time to repent and receive the forgiveness of Christ! Placed before us is life or death. We must choose life to live!"

Amber Matthews, news anchor extraordinaire, didn't seem at all affected by their words but Sophia was quickly reminded that nothing—no-thing—is ever as it seems. Amber quickly said, "It is time for us to turn to our colleagues in the senate floor..."

†

The voting was a roll call vote which meant that every senator's vote would be on record for his or her constituents to see. Since each senator represented a state in which the desires of those who elected him or her were already quite clear, the roll call vote enabled the voters in each state to keep tabs on their elected officials.

As was happening across the European continent, the United States was battling for religious liberties in a way that the Founding Fathers could never have imagined. A nation that once stood proud and strong— even while flawed—now teetered on the brink of extinction.

The presiding officer called the senators alphabetically.

"Jason Abrams."

"Yea."

"Mary Albright."

"Yea."

"Carol Dinetta."

"Yea."

There seemed to be a bit of commotion happening off camera and the viewers quickly realized that it was the crazy senators from Alabama making their to the floor to cast their votes when called upon.

The voting continued.

"Juanita Everman."

"Yea."

"Clyde Grossman"

"Yea."

Sophia remembered in her conversation with her parents that they didn't have a television in Rome so she knew they wouldn't be paying attention to the vote. Nor did Sophia even know if any country other than her own cared about the vote. She considered texting her mom but thought better of it. *This vote isn't going to be much of a surprise so why bring her attention to it? Let her enjoy her time in Rome.*

Instead Sophia sent Jeremy a simple text: I love you. She knew he was in meetings all day; it wasn't about needing him to text her back so that she could see that he loved her, too—because she knew he did. It was about her gratitude that God had given her such a beautiful man to marry. Then, feeling a need to text her mom, Sophia sent her a text, too: Thank you for always praying for me! I love you. After all, she knew her mother certainly had something to do with her upcoming marriage to Jeremy. Sophia knew that her whole life her mother prayed that she would marry a fine young man.

When she was done texting, Sophia joined Julie and Meghan whose attention was now on the action on the senate floor; however, the interior attention of each girl was very much divided. They all knew that Meghan's confession would set them all upon a new path and each was committed to one another like never before. Sophia and Julie would not let Meghan succumb to her depression and Meghan, for her part, would not let go of her friends. God had given her a lifeline and she wasn't about to release it. For the first time in a year, Meghan felt alive again.

"Uriel Rockman."

"Nay."

"Gabriel Slicha."

"Nay."

Well, there it was, the two votes against the bill. The few remaining senators voted in favor of the bill. When the final vote was in, the tally was announced: "We have forty-eight in favor and two against. It is with great pleasure that I am able to announce that the Abortion Rights Tax Act has passed the United States Senate by an overwhelming majority!"

The presiding officer was beside herself, no doubt seeing this a huge step forward for all womankind and for the country as well.

Meghan cried for her country.

Chapter Twenty-Four

*The best approach for reconciling the
being-becoming is simply to try and live it,
without necessarily figuring it out in a
rational or local way.*

~ Carl McColman

The European news stations were ready to run with the story of the historic passage in America of the Abortion Rights Tax Act but the earthquake arising from central Italy put those plans on hold.

Luke and Beth had been enjoying a cup of coffee on their small balcony when they felt the first tremor. Beth had just mentioned that the Abortion Rights Tax Act was being voted upon in the U.S. Senate when she saw the coffee in her coffee cup splash about a bit. Luke looked up and saw what appeared to be dust coming from the brick building across the street. It was barely visible but he could see it nonetheless. The rumble was enough to shake up Beth and to force others out onto their balconies to see what was happening. Beth stood and looked out into the street as people began scurrying into buildings and doorways, very unsure as to what was happening.

In the distance Beth saw—or believed she saw because how could it possibly be?—Miriam. It had been a few years but Meir had been good about keeping in touch and sending a photograph here and there—so proud he was of his beloved daughter.

As Beth watched the familiar figure run towards the Vatican and away from where Beth stood, Beth blurted out in her loud, commanding "mother" voice, "Miriam! Miriam Goldfarb! Up here!"

Miriam stopped in her tracks and quickly turned. She used her hand to shade her eyes to better look up towards the voice that beckoned. Miriam's face looked quizzical as her eyes darted about; then when she spotted Beth on the balcony, her face became one of love and kindness. "Elizabeth? Beth Gantry? Is that truly you?"

"Oh my goodness! No way! How can this even be?" was Beth's stunned response. At this point Luke was on his tip toes leaning over the railing trying to see Miriam but also the commotion that was now growing in the streets.

Miriam took a few steps closer to the building in which Beth and Luke were staying but it was clear that this pained her. She was visibly torn between her friend and whatever it was that was calling her towards the Vatican. It was getting louder and more difficult to communicate. Miriam hoped Beth could hear what she was saying.

"I'm sorry Beth, but I can't come to see you right now. If I am able to see you, I will come back. I hope you are well! How long are you here?"

But Beth could not hear Miriam and simply shrugged her shoulders indicating her inability to make out what Miriam was saying. Miriam held her right hand over her heart and smiled up at Elizabeth. Elizabeth did the same and a tear made its way into the corner of Beth's eye. Before she could blink it away, Miriam was gone.

"Well this sure has been an interesting vacation, hasn't it?" Luke asked as he sat back into his chair. The rumbling had ceased and the people who had sought shelter in the doorways were back on the streets. "That was very strange for you to see your friend from Israel!"

"Yes, but one thing I learned during that trip was that God has a way of making Himself known. I can only imagine what Miriam is doing here but I am convinced that God is asking me to pray for her right now. Do you mind?"

Luke was actually relieved that Beth had suggested they pray. He was more than a bit unsettled at the entire trip thus far and this morning's events only made matters worse. "Sure! Let's go inside. Or would you rather pray out here?"

"I think staying out here is a good idea. I'll just go in and get our rosaries." Within a minute Beth was back on the balcony and their mission as intercessors for Miriam was underway.

"Lord, as we meditate upon the mysteries of Your Son, we offer this rosary to You for Miriam. We ask that our prayers be accepted at Your throne with love and mercy and that Your hand stay upon Miriam."

Beth handed Luke the rosary card so that he could lead and he began, "The first Luminous Mystery. The Baptism of our Lord in the Jordan…"

†

Miriam finished making her way to the Vatican in a sprint. As she wound her way past tourists and natives alike, she heard snippets of conversations.

"What in the world was that?"

"Did you feel that?"

Miriam herself knew that the timing of the minor earthquake and the vote in the US Senate was not a coincidence. In fact, that vote had been the reason that the Four Horsemen project was originally set in motion. Although it had been difficult to determine the exact date of the vote, the project had done a good job— actually Joseph had done an outstanding job—of keeping the task fluid and relevant. He knew that the men desired that their voices be heard in tandem with the outcome of the vote. Joseph's hand was forced with the leak, but it appeared that all had worked out perfectly anyhow. God's timing, as they say. And now the vote was complete. By a landslide the American government had imposed its rule of abortion across the land. Although everyone had been praying for a miracle, they all also prepared for the expected outcome.

Miriam was engulfed in her own thoughts of Beth being in Rome when she rounded the corner and saw the Vatican surrounded by Swiss Guard. That would have been a natural reaction to the earthquake they had all just felt—but which had yet to be confirmed. She approached the Vatican and was met with hostile stares.

Miriam was being asked to liaise between the Vatican and Joseph and this seemed to be a less than opportune time to begin; however, she was a known figure due to her previous work and gave the two guards her Vatican-issued security card. "We cannot let you in today, Ma'am. I'm sorry," was the greeting she received from the head of security.

Miriam knew better than to argue and thanked the man for his time. As she walked away, she could see that the square was being quietly emptied and that barricades were being put in place to keep people and any modes of transportation out of the area. As she continued around the corner she considered heading back to where she had seen Elizabeth; however, Joseph's presence changed that thought.

"Miriam, Shalom!"

"Joseph! What are you doing here?"

"Well, we have Aayan, Abdas, and Abdeel in a secure facility not far from here and I knew that you would not be able to get into the Vatican today so I thought I would ask you to join us."

"Of course I will."

In that moment Miriam had an epiphany. As she looked at Joseph, she knew how much she loved him. Her concern was so much more than that of a colleague; it was that of a lover and a spouse. She had seen it in her parents and knew that it was what she felt for Joseph. She could no longer deny it and its reality— its depth. It was so much more than she had ever imagined. It seems to have existed for eternity and yet was somehow brand new.

More than anything, that realization caused her to remain motionless. She couldn't let this man whom she loved—and had loved for so long—be in this alone.

"Please, let's keep walking," Joseph said as he gingerly put his hand upon Miriam's elbow and guided her along the walk.

"I'm listening," was all Miriam could muster to give Joseph permission to continue on while she sorted through the torrent of her thoughts and emotions.

"Miriam, in reflecting upon the words of White Dove, I have found comfort and a truth. He has encouraged me to have hope in our mission and to not turn back. He has revealed to me the person of Jesus

Christ. This mission has gone from a desire to protect the world from corruption and ruin to a desire to know this man called Christ."

Miriam thought of her friend Elizabeth who had also revealed to Miriam the love of this Jewish man that many called "Lord and Savior" and found she had no response to Joseph. She swallowed hard. She had just made the conscious choice that he would not stand in this alone and he was now declaring a commitment to Jesus. How could she ever follow him now?

These weren't words she wanted to hear in the wake of her own desires but she understood that there was always a chance they would be forthcoming. After all, Joseph's mother was a Christian woman and Miriam had seen firsthand while being part of the Four Horsemen operation how Jesus was the cornerstone of the White Dove's very existence. How ironic that Miriam, herself a Jew, would be assigned to the White Dove while Joffa, a Christian, would be assigned to Abdas and Abdeel, the two rabbis!

Did the omniscient Adonai have a hand in these assignments? Miriam wondered.

Chapter Twenty-Five

Shall I not punish these things? Says the
Lord; on a nation such as this shall I not
take vengeance?

~Jeremiah 5:29

As Joseph and Miriam made their way back to the secure location where Abdul was guarding Aayan and Joffa was watching over Abdas and Abdeel, he continued talking. Trying to explain, really, what he knew Miriam was having a very difficult time grasping.

"God is at work right now and no one—not even you, sweet Miriam—has the luxury of time."

Miriam's heart fluttered at the term of endearment that Joseph used. It was as if all the walls that had ever been built up between them to keep their professional life safe and secure were now tumbling down. And the moment couldn't have been more inopportune.

At that Miriam asked, "What do you mean we don't have the luxury of time? That sounds quite ominous, Joseph!"

"You see, Miriam, as I said, this has gone from a task—an assignment—to a personal invitation from God to know Jesus. To accept Jesus. It seems rather unproductive to work this way but I guess that is how it goes. In my mind I would think that a whole lot more could be accomplished if hundreds and tens of hundreds of people would come to know Christ at one time; but having been part of this Four Horsemen mission I can see that it is a very personal, very private experience. Sure, lots of people can be converted but it will be because each has been in relationship with someone else and that person will have introduced this man Jesus. It is all about relationship.

"I can tell someone all I want about the power of Christ's forgiveness, let's say, but if I have no relationship with the person to whom I am speaking, then I am, as they say, a clanging gong.

"It's all about love. First ours with Christ and then ours with one another."

"In Hebrew this is called 'yachasim,'" Miriam said as she thought about her brother's love for Hashem and his love for others. "It is about relationship—ours with each other and ours with God. My brother David is a wonderful man whose love for the Most Blessed One is vital to everything—all facets of his life; so much so that anyone who knows David ends up loving their Creator all the more—or even loving Him for the first time. That is because David is in right relationship with God and God brings to David's life people who will see that right relationship and desire it for themselves."

Yes, what Joseph was saying made perfect sense. She also thought about al-tiv'i—the Jewish teaching on the supernatural—and knew that the ancestors in her faith had lived a life in which the curtain between earth and Heaven was thin and was often pulled back. *Why shouldn't God be pulling it back right now?* she wondered. *If ever there was a time in which the power of Hashem was needed in the world, it is in the present days.*

Thinking of her own prayers and finding a new trust in them—and in the real presence of God—she said, "So, what does all this mean for the project? I guess I'm a little confused as to what you are saying."

"Well, first things first. The project is moving forward and we are to get our charges to their final destination this morning for their news conference. The vote is in for the U.S. Senate and the message of the Four Horsemen is now paramount. They have been working all morning on it and it is now up to us to deliver them safely to the place in which they feel their words will have the most impact: the Colosseum where so many shed their blood.

"After that, it is time for you and I to discuss our own relationship. We've danced around this long enough; we've put up barriers that now need to be taken down. It is time for us to be honest with ourselves and with one another."

Miriam smiled as she and Joseph picked up their pace. The remainder of their time together was spent in silence—and in eager anticipation.

Chapter Twenty-Six

*Then Satan entered into Judas, the one
surnamed Iscariot, who was counted
among the Twelve.*

~ Luke 22:3

As Miriam and Joseph gathered White Dove, Aayan, Abdas, and Abdeel together, a few polizia secured the way towards the vehicle that would take them all to the Colosseum. The minor trembling from the morning's apparent earthquake did little to squelch the enthusiasm of the tourists who were filling the streets and taking in all the sights. As the van pulled up to the Colosseum and let the remnants of the group disembark, there was a loud shriek in the street.

A woman's purse was stolen and people were running in all directions; some to offer help while others were meant to provide cover for the perpetrator. Street crime was quite common in Rome but this incident was a bit different. The commotion it caused was meant as a distraction but it did little in the way of deterring what the four men were about to do.

Joseph had contacted local networks and reporters who had been scheduled to cover the news conference but who now had other, more important topics to occupy their time. The minor earthquake was still under investigation with seismologists not quite willing to confirm the quake or its final magnitude.

The manslaughter conviction of a number of Italian seismologists a few years back for not adequately predicting an earthquake forever changed the way in which the field of study was practiced and how subsequent data was disseminated. The tragedy happened in the city of L'Aquila and left more than 300 people dead. To add to the tragedy, the Italian government's decision to convict the seismologists of manslaughter was seen as further damage. The head of the Italian disaster recovery arm resigned in protest but the damage had already been done. The conviction had permanently changed the field; the result was that it now had everyone fearful of what they said—and did not say. It was a catastrophe on so many levels.

Today's tremors bore witness to the damage that the entire L'Aquila event brought to the region: the physical as well as the emotional.

No doubt the press smelled a bigger story in what they would undoubtedly dub a cover-up since no warning had come to the residents of the city prior to the tremors. Joseph had to thus play the cards he was dealt and proceeded to make phone calls on his cell while they drove to their destination. It would certainly take a miracle for the press to attend this meeting of the religious leaders with the earthquake story growing bigger as the day wore on.

Chapter Twenty-Seven

*But Abraham replied, "They have Moses
and the prophets. Let them listen to them."*

*He said, "Oh no, father Abraham, but if
someone from the dead goes to them, they
will repent."*

*Then Abraham said, "If they will not listen
to Moses and the prophets, neither will
they be persuaded if someone should rise
from the dead.*

~ Luke 16:29-31

Stepping from the van, the first thing that Abdul noticed was that the camera's lights were far brighter than he imagined they would be. He immediately stepped in between them and Aayan while Joseph and Miriam flanked Aayan on both sides. Questions were being shouted from the crowd but Aayan remained calm. He did not look up nor did he look directly into anyone's eyes. He was clearly in prayer.

Next out of the van was White Dove. Abdas and Abdeel quickly followed. Together they all stepped behind the threesome of Joseph, Miriam, and Aayan. Joffa was the last to emerge from the vehicle and kept his eyes darting from camera to microphone back to camera as he surveyed the crowd. Joseph had not requested additional help within the Colosseum. He had been confident that they would be able to escort the four clerics into the Colosseum without incident and then proceed as planned. He hadn't expected that the reporters would have shown up in the numbers that they did and so was caught quite by surprise. This is what we wanted, he told himself, as they all walked in tandem towards their destination within the Colosseum.

The cameras continued to record the small group, questions continued to be thrown at the clerics, and security threats began to rise. In the corner of his eye, Joseph caught someone running from the Colosseum and just as he was about to ask Joffa if he had also seen this action, Joffa came around to Joseph's side to make mention of it.

"It can't be good," was all Joffa said. Then his eyes moved in the direction of the man Joseph had just seen and he added, "That man running from the Colosseum. We must assume that he has set something up based upon information he has purchased from the agent who has betrayed our mission. We ought to immediately abort."

Joseph felt torn.

While he knew Jaffa was correct in the statement that the mission should be aborted, Joseph also knew that there would never be another time such as this to warn the world of the real impending danger that lurked just around the corner.

Almost against his better judgment, Joseph said, "While you are right, Joffa, I know that we must proceed with the Four Horsemen assignment. Now is our time to serve both God and country, come what may. Now is our time to make the truth known to the nations. These men have committed their lives to God and have freely offered themselves as such. They are willing to die for the truth and we cannot take that from them—or from God."

Joffa could only agree; there was no point arguing with the leader as this would merely reduce their strength exponentially. Now the only thing to do would be to stand against whatever was about to happen inside the stone walls and bleachers of the great Colosseum. *It won't be the first time these walls have seen blood* were Jaffa's sobering thoughts as he stepped inside the ruins.

As they moved forward, throngs of people filed in behind them. Many were already inside and within minutes all the men and the agents were in the center of the vast ring. Joseph thought about the White Dove's last words to him this morning as they prepared for this moment:

"Do not be afraid to give your life for your friends. This, too, is what Jesus has done. He tells us that there is no greater love than to give one's life for a friend and then He does just: He gives His life for us all."

†

Beth and Luke were in the stands of the crowded Colosseum, having been more or less pulled in by the zealous crowds. Instead of fighting against them and risk being trampled, Luke said, "Come on Beth, let's see what's going on. It must be something big since it looks like all the news crews and reporters are here. Maybe they are going to talk about the earthquake—or maybe there is word about the pope's health." While Luke wasn't quite buying the story that the pope had suddenly come down with the flu, he felt it was his duty not to spread gossip or add to anyone's fears. Beth also felt there was more to it than that but remained silent on the subject. It didn't do anyone any good to speculate.

She thought about the text from Sophia and felt buoyed with optimism, "Sure. Let's do that. Just don't lose me!"

Luke chuckled and grabbed hold of Beth's hand. He squeezed it rather hard until he saw Beth's face grimace. "Sorry 'bout that," he said and then loosened his grip—but just by a hair. They didn't come this far in their marriage—and fly half way around the world—to get separated in the ominous surroundings of the Colosseum.

Finding an empty spot, Beth and Luke nestled into each other's side and focused on what was taking place. The crowd was noisy and appeared to have no interest in listening to the young man who was trying to speak. Beth squinted and silently chastised herself for not having grabbed her glasses off the counter. Next to the young man speaking was a young woman who looked an awful lot like Miriam. Luke was busy looking over the crowds and finding an easy way out when Beth nudged him. "Is that woman down there Miriam? The one I called out to from our balcony this morning?"

"Wow! Yes, it sure is!" replied an astonished Luke. "Imagine that!"

He turned to Beth with questions that she clearly did not have answers to and just as she did this morning to Miriam, Beth looked at Luke and shrugged her shoulders. They both then turned towards the handful of people who were clearly the reason they were all here.

Someone handed the young man a microphone and he began speaking:

"Thank you, ladies and gentlemen of the press, for taking the time to respond to our request for a news conference. As I shared with each of you earlier, this is a matter of international importance. Gathered today are four men who represent different religious institutions."

Everyone looked around at each other. Joseph now had their attention. While they didn't necessarily know who the Muslim cleric was nor did they know the rabbis, they certainly knew their pope! A murmur ran through the crowd as they all wondered why these men had gathered in this place.

When his Excellency raised his hand and made the sign of the cross for the crowd, many of those who had gathered were signing themselves and whispering prayers. These were the believers to whom the task would fall: these were the ones who were transformed by the miraculous and would become instruments of hope and change for the world. These were the anointed who responded to Christ's call and who understood that while they lived *in* the world, they were not *of* the world.

†

Beth and Luke were counted among the believers and as they made the sign of the cross, Beth looked up into the skies above the gathering. To her left she noticed that the clouds had taken on a formation. It looked as if the sky was filling with beautiful, white angels and Beth tugged on Luke's sleeve and nodded towards the formation. Luke looked up and smiled back at Elizabeth not quite understanding what she was seeing but noticing that whatever it was, it gave her joy. His gaze returned to the center of the stadium while Elizabeth continued to look heavenward. She could hardly believe what she was seeing, though she had not averted her eyes even for an instance. The skies above the Colosseum were now filled with heavenly host. Countless angels clad in white were descending from the heavens. The sight was unlike anything Beth had ever seen and her heart pounded within her chest.

Her mind raced with Scripture verses as her eyes continued to feast upon the beauty in the skies. Beth stood outside of time and space and simply kept her gaze upon the heavenly messengers. She remembered hearing, once, a sermon preached wherein the priest talked about miracles. He said the reason we don't experience miracles is because we no longer expected them. We had become jaded and were all too quick to call something a coincidence rather than give God credit for pulling back the curtain and entering into our lives in a meaningful way. After listening to that priest, Elizabeth became a person who expected miracles. Big or small, it did not matter. Her life had been more rewarding because of it and now, well, now all she could think was that God was allowing her to experience a much larger miracle because she had been obedient in the small things. *Wasn't that what life was about: being obedient in the small ways? How could God give us the bigger gifts and rewards if we weren't doing a good job with the small ones?* It seemed like a silly, remedial way to approach faith but for Beth it made sense and had worked. It had blessed her with many of God's consolations in the years since that homily.

As Beth waited for the miraculous appearance of Jesus in the midst of the angels, what happened next almost stopped her beating heart. As the skies filled with the angels of light and love, so too did it begin to fill with dark, foreboding angels. To her right, Miriam noticed them arriving from a distance and at first could not make out the dark shadows that were rapidly approaching. Within seconds, though, it became clear that the angels of light would not be alone in the sky; the angels of darkness now came upon the crowds as well.

Beth frantically looked around. No one, not a single person, seemed to be seeing what she was seeing. She refused to let fear overcome her remembering the words of one of her favorite popes, John Paul II. He had said, just as Christ had said, "Do not be afraid." Elizabeth latched onto those words and refused to give in to her fears. Quietly, she heard herself say "It has begun" and caught a glimpse of Luke staring quizzically at her. She fortuitously remembered that the day after Christmas was the Feast of St. Stephen, the first martyr to die for the faith. How important to now see this connection. She understood, then, the dark angels; you could not have the angels of light and love and not have the dark angels as well. Quickly she prayed that everyone present would be covered in the precious blood of Christ.

†

"I hope you are getting all this!" growled one woman reporter to her cameraman as she watched the pope make the sign of the cross. The reporter wasn't so much transfixed by the events taking place before her very eyes as much as she was inspired by the thought of a Pulitzer Prize.

"Yeah. Yeah. I got it all," replied the beleaguered man as he panned the audience and then focused the camera back onto the people standing in the middle of the ancient stadium.

One of the rabbis stepped forward. It had been determined that just as St. Paul said that God's plan was "Jew first, then Gentile" it would be best way to honor God by having the rabbi read the statement that had been jointly prepared by the four men. It was in one of seven envelopes that were being held. The Four Horsemen each held a sealed envelope and each of the body guards—minus Joseph and Miriam—held one as well. There were to be seven proclamations that day.

The first began as the rabbi broke the seal and opened the envelope. In perfect English he began:

"May the God of Abraham, Isaac, Jacob, and Joseph be blessed and bless us. May He shine His light upon us today in our hour of darkness. May He enlighten us with wisdom, inspire us with love, and fortify us with strength.

"Our call is to bring light to the world. Many people today consider these very words to be arrogant—to be rude and intrusive; yet that is not the case.

"Our call is to reveal eternal truths to the world. Many people today consider these very words to be hypocritical and folly as they are often delivered by men of sin, men who have themselves transgressed; yet that very fact does not diminish the need for eternal truths. Indeed, it confirms it!

"Our call is to invite everyone to repentance."

At this the crowd jostled against each other uneasily. Eyes were downcast and hearts seemed heavy. The rabbi was speaking the truth in that men do not like to be told things in a blatant or bold way. But for all the movement, no one left the Colosseum. The rabbi continued.

"In Hebrew we call repentance by the word 'teshuvah.' It means 'to turn around in order to return.' We also have an immersion in water which we call 'tevilah b'mayim.' There was a Jewish man named John whom many called 'The Baptist.' He lived in the desert and cried out for repentance and tevilah b'mayim—which many now call baptism. John was announcing the need for people to recognize their sinful ways and change their behavior. They had to turn around from the path that they were on so that they could return to

God, blessed be His holy name. Many did not like hearing John's message just as many don't like to hear messages of light and truth today.

"In Hebrew we have a word for 'individual.' It is 'ishi.' I am standing before you speaking to thousands but God is calling each of us individually. He doesn't want even one of us lost to evil and destruction. God desires each of us to be with Him for eternity; but first we have to make a decision. We have to respond to John's message of repentance as if it were being said to us today. That is our message as we stand before you.

"Make no mistake about it: John's message is as important in our day as it was when he heralded it thousands of years ago! He wanted people to see that their behavior was taking them away from God. A God who loved them individually and longed for their return! Even though John's message was unpopular, he could not stop saying it. Everyone needed to know that God was not at the end of the road upon which they were traveling.

"And now we need to know the same thing! Don't be misled! I beg you! God is not at the end of the road we are on, either. Just like the people did when John called them to repent, so, too, must we turn around in order to return to God!"

With each new sentence, the rabbi's voice increased an octave. In some ways he could have been John the Baptist. His message was strong and clear—and unpopular; for as many believers that filled the stands, so, too, were the number of unbelievers. Or, as Beth more correctly thought: these people aren't unbelievers as much as they were people whose faith has become so watered down that there was no room for God; they have created their own faith, so to speak.

Someone from the crowd yelled out, "Yeah? And what if we don't?"

There were a number of hecklers who liked that question and chimed in as well.

"Come on, man! What do we do that's so wrong?"

And another stated what many felt was the obvious, "Compared to most people, I'm a saint!"

Beth doubted that the rabbi heard any of these queries as the crowds were huge and the questions weren't asked in front of a microphone or amplifier.

Beth suddenly remembered a Scripture verse that she had always found unsettling: "For I have come to set a man against his father, and a daughter against her mother, and a daughter-in-law against her mother-in-law; and a man's foes will be those of his own household." *Is this what Jesus meant when he said he would turn brother against brother, father against son?* It all seemed to make perfect sense now as they stood amid the throngs of people.

Elizabeth recalled the charged conversations that she and Sophia had been involved in over the past few years—this was why Beth knew this verse by heart. She remembered the first time she heard it and felt absolutely baffled. Her immediate response was, *Shouldn't Christ bring families together? Shouldn't Christ bring harmony?*

At the time, she couldn't understand how conversations with her daughter—and she used the word "conversations" in its most liberal sense—could always end up with Sophia huffing off and slamming a door which was meant to give the final, non-verbal assertion that Elizabeth truly understood nothing! Beth could now see that it wasn't that Christ purposely wanted to divide families—or churches or disciples or believers—but rather that He knew this would be the outcome as people made decisions to "follow Him." And not just follow Him in an esoteric way; but truly follow Him in the way that Simon and his brother Andrew—and then James and John—followed Jesus when He invited them to become "fishers of men."

Your life just couldn't be the same after making such a decision; if it remained the same then the decision hadn't been real or substantial, Beth concluded not too many years ago. She loved the story of these men. There they were, Simon and Andrew, going about their business by the Sea of Galilee, when Jesus walks by. They are in the middle of casting their nets—earning their living, going about their business—and Jesus says "Follow me, and I will make you fishers of men." *Astounding!* thought Elizabeth; but she knew that this was exactly how it happened. *And you can either accept the invitation or reject it. It is all up to you.*

This is why Elizabeth and Sophia would fight about things of faith. In the old days, before Elizabeth made the commitment to Christ—before she dropped her net and followed Him—she preferred to keep the peace at home and would let Sophia have her say or her thoughts. Now, the more Beth learned about the teachings of Christ and the truths behind them all, the less she could let Sophia just skirt an issue with her common sense view of things or her desire to see the world become a better, "more tolerant," place. *Ah, youth!* Beth thought to herself all the while praying that Sophia would soon drop her own net and follow Christ. The best bumper sticker Beth ever saw was the one that said: You can be so open-minded that your brains will fall out.

How true, indeed.

Now, as the crowds pushed against one another bristling at the words of the rabbi, Elizabeth's epiphany about that verse was complete. A definite "Aha!" moment but not one that brought peace or relief; it was an "Aha!" moment that brought in its wake a bit of sadness derived from the knowledge that the road ahead would be a bumpy one, to be sure.

Elizabeth's attention returned to center stage as Joseph took charge and raised his hand for silence. "This time in our lives that brings together people of all faiths is a time of challenge. These men here," and with that Joseph held out his right hand, palm up, and gestured towards the four clerics, "These men here care more about your souls than their own lives. They care more about your eternal life than they do their earthly lives. That should be clear to you by their very gathering. They put everything at risk to be here today.

"They understand that it is easy to mock and dismiss; but each ask that their flock take to heart the message brought to you here today—a dark day in the United States and thus a dark day in the world."

Beth and Luke looked at each other and knew then that the vote had been counted and that the Abortion Rights Tax Act had passed. Beth cried but she wasn't quite sure why. Everyone knew that this was, after all, a foregone conclusion. However, the tears made their appearance nonetheless. Maybe it was the way that people dismissed the truth that life began at conception; maybe it was because she longed to hold her babies just one more time. Whatever it was, it caught her a bit by surprise but she let it have its escape. Her spiritual director had recently told Beth that the tears she often shed were tears of the spirit and this could very well have been one of those times. Tears for the lives that would be taken with this new legislation; tears for the lives that had already been taken.

Mother Teresa had said at a National Prayer Breakfast in the late 1990s that what was happening in America was a war on children. Beth couldn't quite remember the exact quote but it was a chilling indictment of where America had been and was headed—and now it would be exponentially worse with this new legislation. Beth combed her mind for the words; something to the effect that you can't let mothers kill their own children and then tell other people they can't kill!

As Beth recalled that insightful message, she saw that Joseph took a step back and the other rabbi shuffled forward. He seemed far older than his apparent years. *An old soul,* Beth thought to herself. She wasn't sure if he would have the stamina to make whatever statement was his to make so when with trembling hands he broke the seal of his envelope and began speaking, she was taken aback. His voice was young and vibrant and full of life.

"There was a man named Saul. A Jewish man. A man who loved his faith and who defended it against the many who were seen to be an affront to that faith. He persecuted them and he drove them from their homes and cities and businesses. He did this all for God—his God.

"Then one day Saul met a man named Jesus. Jesus wanted to know why Saul was persecuting him. This meeting took place on the road to Damascus. My friend just spoke to you about the road you are on, the road many of us are on. Well, Saul was on a road, too, and Hashem, blessed be His Holy Name, wanted to get Saul off that road.

"And God wasn't subtle about it."

Those believers in the stands who knew the story of St. Paul being knocked down by a flashing, blinding light chuckled as if to say, *"Yep, sometimes God uses big ways to get our attention!"*

The rabbi continued, "Saul became a different man after that meeting. He understood more fully what it meant to serve God—to know God's truths and to want to live in those truths.

"Saul became Paul. The Paul that many of you know about and have read about. Paul was as passionate about his newfound relationship with this man Jesus as he was when he was Saul and was defending the God of Abraham, Isaac, Jacob, and Joseph.

"Today we are all on the road to Damascus. We are being asked to make radical changes within ourselves. Imagine how much Saul changed that he needed a new name! We must be willing to make changes such as these. Changes in which our old names no longer identify who we are!

"We are being asked to know God in a personal, intimate way that will forever change each of us. Jews are invited to know this man Jesus and Gentiles are invited to meet the Father, Adonai. We all have much in common; but make no mistake about it: we are being invited to change our ways and to become new men and women of faith.

"As Jews we begin our day in prayer. We pray the *Amidah* and we pray the *Sh'ma*. Let me offer the *Sh'ma* for us now.

"Sh'ma Yis'ra'eil Adonai Eloheinu Adonai echad. This means, 'Hear, Israel, the Lord is our God, the Lord is One.' And he is one! He is the Creator of us all!"

Luke was very much taken with the rabbi's message of change. The visualization of being on a road was quite profound. He thought back to the early years of his marriage to Beth in which they both wanted the other to change. They were on very different roads. They each believed that their unhappiness came from the other; that the other just needed to get on the right road. But they were unwilling—or unable—to recognize that happiness and peace come from within and that they each needed to turn around so that they could return to their marriage.

They each had to radically change, just as Saul did, to save what was left of their marriage. It took many years to fully discover that it wasn't about Luke making certain changes to please Beth and vice-versa. No, it was about interior changes—getting on the right road—that then changed the course of their marriage and their relationship. Luke watched as the second rabbi took a step back and Joseph moved forward. Luke surmised that Joseph would be introducing the next ecclesiastic to speak but it wasn't clear if it would be the pope or the Muslim cleric. It was difficult to tell but from Luke's vantage point it looked like everyone except the young man who seemed to be, essentially, emceeing the gathering—and Miriam—had an envelope in hand. Their messages had mesmerized Luke; they felt so personal, and now he looked forward to the next one.

No sooner did that thought enter and leave Luke's mind when blasts were heard around the stands. They sounded like the rudimentary fireworks that Luke and the kids used to light on the 4th of July. Luke craned his head around, as did Beth, trying to find the source of the blasts that were now spurting up all around them and causing panic in the stands.

†

Miriam had stood her place in the center of the rather large, almost unwieldy event. In some ways it seemed rather ludicrous that the four of them—Joseph included—were to keep the Four Horsemen safe against any potential threat or violence that may occur. One good group of people could easily stampede the eight of them as they stood almost as intentional targets. Miriam's eyes continued to dart up and down and all around the crowds. Mostly, though, Miriam reflected on what was being said by the men. She thought about her own life and the lives of her parents and her brother. She still struggled with the death of her mother and knew that her father and brother did as well. *Does anyone really ever get over the death of a loved one?* Miriam wondered. Death was all around her and not one of them ever left her unaffected. Each soul that she encountered was a soul she longed to protect. Her mother once lovingly said that this desire of Miriam's to protect everyone had always been Miriam's way, even from when she was a little child. Miriam's focus was on the classmate who didn't have friends or the neighbor who ate alone. From a tender age Miriam had a heart for the downtrodden, the broken, the neglected.

Now, here she was, protecting others once again; but against what, she was unsure. Abdas spoke of repentance and Miriam thought of all the ways in which she may have failed her mother while her mother was alive. Of course she knew that in the end, there were no harsh words or feelings between them; but that didn't always keep guilt at bay. Miriam could still be caught in its claws on days where her sorrow was too much to bear. Miriam knew her own faults and made a firm commitment to get on the right road—as Abdeel had said. Miriam wanted to be on the road that led to God and not on the road that led to her own version of truth or faith or life.

She looked at Joseph and felt her heart flutter. *What did he say earlier? We've been doing this dance far too long?* Miriam was flooded with feelings of love for Joseph and looked forward to tomorrow, a new day in which they could be on the same road: a road towards a future that she knew would include marriage and children. She remembered watching a television show once where a woman was faced with a decision to marry or to make a career move which would have left her lover behind. When the woman made her decision to follow the career opportunity she had said, "This is a once in a lifetime chance."

Miriam reacted physically to hearing those words, sadness filling her heart. How could a woman not see love as a "once-in-a-lifetime" opportunity? Careers can come and go; but people with whom we can spend our lives with may only come along once in a lifetime. Miriam knew then that should she ever be faced with such a decision, it would be simple: Miriam would choose love and family over career and never look back.

Joseph was now that man and Miriam was completely prepared to forge a life with him. She trusted God would guide them as they tackled Joseph's revelation that he was enamored with Christ. She didn't know what it would mean; but she had confidence in God. After all, she couldn't honestly reflect on the last couple of days and deny His existence and involvement in her life and the lives of others. He had never been more real to her than at this moment in time.

Just then odd popping sounds started erupting in the stands. People were gasping, looking around—everyone was bewildered. That included the eight of them on the grounds of the Colosseum until they realized that it was a clever diversion from something that was about to happen. Joseph instantly knew who had set up the now-popping caps: the man who had purchased information from the rogue agent, the same man who they had seen fleeing from the Colosseum as they were arriving. Joseph also knew, in the depths of his heart, why...and what was going to happen next.

At first, the bodyguards made an effort to herd the men to safety but were stopped by their collective stance. They all began praying. The pope knelt down and made the sign of the cross, the rabbis began rocking back and forth and Aayan lay prostrate on the ground. In different tongues, prayers rose to the heavens. The angels of light that had gathered stood guard while the angels of darkness prowled through the crowds searching for a weakened spirit, a defeated soul, a damaged man who would be easy prey. The spiritual battle was being taken to a new level and all were players, whether they realized it or not.

Miriam, Abdul, and Joffa each remained vigilant and yet helpless. *What were they to do?* Miriam wondered. She had never had a charge of hers deny her protection. These men were laying down their lives for God. Unlike terrorists who brought death and destruction, these men became willing victims if death and destruction were on its way.

At the very same time, training being what it was, both Miriam and Joseph noticed a glint of metal in the deepest recesses of the stands; up and to their right. Miriam called out to the others just as Joseph made the purposeful decision to stand in front of the Muslim cleric; to become a human shield. All their intel seemed to indicate that there would be two targets this day: White Dove and Aayan. Since White Dove had revealed to Joseph the night before that Aayan would be in grave danger, Joseph's split-second decision was to protect Aayan.

No one heard the shot and no one immediately noticed—except Miriam. She stepped towards Joseph just in time to catch him. Within seconds, screams erupted in the stands and masses of people ran towards the exits. With no thought of anyone else, the crowds pushed their way to safety. People were being trampled and the confusion continued to escalate. Outside the Colosseum sirens were heard. Someone had shown the good sense to call for help.

Holding Joseph in her arms, with blood rushing out from a wound in his chest, Miriam assured him, "Help is only moments away! Please, I beg you to hold on! Do not leave me now! We have a whole life to live."

Joseph gave Miriam a weak smile and moved his lips. She bent over him to better hear what he was attempting to say. She had torn off her jacket and was now holding it on his wound but the blood was soaking through at an alarming rate. The pain Miriam felt in her chest was unbearable; it was as if she was being crushed and for a moment she imagined she was having a heart attack—*because how much pain could one heart take?*—and yet she willingly accepted that fate. She waited to be gunned down as well. She even found solace in the idea of dying while holding Joseph in her arms. As her mind filled with such thoughts, she also wondered about life after death. She felt ready.

In the midst of the chaos Miriam felt a hand upon her shoulder. It was the White Dove. He simply smiled at her. His eyes invited hers into a depth of love that she never knew existed. This was the love of Christ that Joseph had told her about. In that moment she knew that Christ Himself was inviting her home. She thought of the dream she had of her mother the night before and remembered that her mother called her a "beloved daughter of the Most High God." Now, in the depths of the pope's gaze, Miriam understood that truth.

Her body was flooded with a sense of peace and calm. The shooter must have considered himself successful, or had abandoned his mission. Either way, Miriam had not been harmed. She came fully back into the present moment and looked lovingly into Joseph's eyes. They seemed to be focused on something in the distance and Miriam wondered if he, too, were imagining their life together in a place beyond this present moment.

Just as Miriam's attention had been brought back to the current situation, so, too, was Joseph's. In a stronger voice than he had previously possessed he said to her, "Your father has something for you from me."

Miriam only responded with a quizzical look, wondering what he could be talking about and assuming he was hallucinating. She remained silent and prayed that the look that was in her eyes mirrored the love she had for him in her heart: Christ's love.

If Joseph had more to say, she wanted him to know that he could say it with freedom and that every word he uttered would be cherished by her all the days of her life.

"Please tell my parents how very much I love them. And my sisters. They all know my intentions and how very much I have loved you from the very start. I'm only sorry that it took us so long to get to this point. Forgive me."

Forgiveness. What a beautiful gift they had all been given. A gift received and a gift meant to give. She said, "There is nothing for which you should apologize—or which needs to be forgiven. Maybe it is I that ought to beg forgiveness! How did I let all our time pass without proclaiming my love? But I see that ours was a friendship that turned to love and that is the best kind of love to have!"

Joseph smiled almost imperceptibly and said, "So you love me, too?"

Miriam didn't feel as if she had been breathing for the past five minutes and with Joseph's question she gasped so deeply that even Joseph noticed. "Of course I do! You have been the love of my life for as long as I have known you!" The words were filled with a truth that Miriam only seemed to fully recognize once she had uttered them. As she thought about them she watched as Joseph's eyes slowly closed. She did not plead for him to hold on as she knew this was just not possible. Instead, she let the last words he heard be the ones of a love proclaimed.

Angels ushered Joseph to his eternal reward in heaven as Miriam held onto this lifeless body.

†

Miriam had held Joseph as he let go of life. His entire shirt front was covered in blood. How ironic, she thought, that his heart should become so visible to her in this way. As her eyes fixed themselves upon Joseph's face she heard the chaos in the Colosseum and gave a furtive look into the sky. Miriam noticed what seemed to be angels hovering over many people. Some seemed cloaked in white while others were covered in gray material—or had what seemed like a dark, boding aura clinging to their fluid bodies. Surely her eyes were playing tricks on her as her heart ached for Joseph and she tried to coax her mind into thinking like a Mossad agent.

Miriam recalled praying the *Amidah*. She thought of Joseph's bold words about Christ. She contemplated the wind that swept through the catacombs that night in Rome—*could it have been just a couple of nights ago?* All these thoughts bombarded her as she did her best to let her training kick in. She remembered Judge Deborah, the warrior and prophetess.

Miriam knew that she was being called to the front lines of a supernatural battle that was taking place in the natural world. This was the time for action. God counted on people to take action—to be warriors—and Miriam was forcing herself to think clearly, to think like a warrior.

Yet she couldn't quite get her racing mind and pounding heart to obey. She wanted to be lifted out of the nightmare that was taking place and be placed in a world where tears did not exist. She longed for a time when her heart would not hammer inside her chest wall with pain but would gently beat with love and peace. Miriam ached for a life in which fear and anxiety were not permanent residences in the deep recesses of her mind, never knowing what the next minute or hour or day would hold. As doubt filled her mind and dread took hold of her heart she wondered, *Was Joseph now in that place of love and peace? Was Joseph with the Creator? Was Christ welcoming Joseph who, like Jesus, gave his life for another?*

Miriam looked at Joseph. She held him tight in her arms, his lifeless, limp body lying across her lap. Against all Jewish precepts of touching the dead, she ran the back of her hand across his clean-shaven face. He was still warm to the touch as she murmured "Ani Leh'dodi Veh'dodli Li."

†

As Abdul and Joffa walked their charges towards one of the stone doorways of the crumbling Colosseum, each was painfully aware that Joseph had given his life just as so many had done in the days of Roman persecution. *How many had died within these walls?* each man wondered silently while offering a prayer for God's guidance amidst the turmoil which was surrounding them. People were running and screaming giving no apparent care or concern for their fellow man; Joseph lay dead in Miriam's arms, White Dove had been taken to safety by his own guards. No amount of training could have prepared them for what they had experienced. Nonetheless, protocol called for them to usher Aayan, Abdas, and Abdeel to the predetermined location which was supposed to provide safety—although no one felt sure of this anymore. In the distance, against the backdrop of fleeing people, the agents watched as two men and a woman worked their way into the stadium carrying a stretcher. Out of the corner of their eyes they watched as Miriam's head hung slightly over Joseph's face. Clearly heartbroken, Miriam was whispering words that were meant for Joseph alone.

†

As Miriam whispered her words of love to Joseph, her mind floated back to the previous Passover. As was the custom during that week, her father read Shir Ha-Shirim—King Solomon's ancient love song, the *Song of Songs*. Although it had been a number of years since Ayala's death, the practice did not cease in the Goldfarb home; indeed, it became all the sweeter to contemplate love since Meir and Ayala's affection had been so enduring. Just as it should, their marriage reflected—at its very core—a Jew's romance with God. And that was what the *Song of Songs* was all about: recalling God's great love for his people during Passover when the Jews marked their doorposts with the blood of a lamb thereby avoiding the death that was visited upon the firstborn sons of the Egyptians. Chag Ha-Aviv—

Passover—was the springtime celebration of innovation, imagination, inspiration, and expectancy.

Miriam loved thinking about this, the greatest song of all which tells the story of the greatest love affair of all: the love affair between God and The People of the Book. Scholars had differing opinions about the actual author of the famous tale of love but all agreed that this—the first scroll of the five that composed the *Megillah* (the story of Esther)—was about the marriage of the Jewish people to their God during the time of Exodus.

Miriam even recalled Elizabeth sharing her own knowledge about the *Song of Solomon*. Elizabeth and Miriam had spent a morning over coffee reveling in the ways in which their faiths were connected. Indeed, the reason Beth had travelled from the United States to Israel had been due to her fascination with the Jewish roots of her Christian faith. So on the one hand they shouldn't have been so surprised to uncover instance after instance in which the Jewish Messiah was made known—and yet on the other hand they couldn't help but marvel at what was being revealed through their conversation. The *Song of Songs* was only one of many examples of how the Jewish faith fed the Christian faith and now Miriam was recalling how Beth had spoken of this great love story as the love of Jesus and his bride, the Church. At the thought of Beth, Miriam's heart flooded with love and concern. *Was Beth here today? Was she safe?*

As if guided by an unseen force, Miriam's mind let go of those concerns and drifted back to the *Song of Songs* where she remembered learning that Maimonides, the great Jewish scholar, was adamant that the search for the Beloved written about was to reflect each person's own search for HaShem. In the same way that the rabbi had just told the crowd, it was an individual love—an individual relationship with each of us. The seeking and the finding was something that God intended.

Miriam recalled how Beth had likened it to an Easter egg hunt. She told Miriam that she and Luke hid Easter eggs and loved when their kids went about the house on Easter morning looking for the hidden eggs. They were filled with excitement and enthusiasm—just as Beth and Luke were at the idea of each child finding any number of eggs. "That," Beth said to Miriam, "was what a relationship with God is all about. He wants us to search and to find. He invites us to go into deep and seemingly hidden places but that is where the best treasures exist! Just like Luke and I don't want the eggs to remain hidden and get rotten, neither does our Heavenly Father want His gifts to be left undiscovered."

The teacher in Beth always shone when she explained things. Miriam had listened eagerly as Beth continued and spoke of the lilies in the song and explained to Miriam the significance of lilies. "Some people call lilies 'white-robed apostles of hope.' They were supposed to have been found in the Garden of Gethsemane which certainly makes them significant." Beth's enthusiasm was always evident when she shared with Miriam these discoveries she had made in her own search for God. She continued explaining to Miriam how significant white was as it symbolized purity and expectation. "And, according to legend," Beth continued, "when it was time to select a husband for Mary, all the men were asked to lay their staffs on the ground and Joseph's miraculously bloomed like a lily. That is why St. Joseph is always seen holding lilies!"

Beth had waited for Miriam's enthusiasm at that fact to make itself evident before she continued. Miriam obliged and raised her eyebrows and giggled at Beth who was talking like a schoolgirl who had just learned that the cute boy in school liked her! Once Beth noted Miriam's enthusiastic response she went on, "In fact, somewhere in Scripture is the phrase—now let me get this right—'A just man will blossom like a lily!'" As they continued to talk about lilies and love and the deep places in which God was found, they also spoke of the way in which Easter and Passover shared springtime as their time of celebration.

Yes, Beth had been correct about it all. The *Song of Songs* was about the anxious, excited anticipation of discovering our beloved. Unfortunately, it was also a tale of unfaithfulness on the part of the young bride. What began at Passover—the engagement of God and His people—ended with the infidelity on the part of the People of the Book. They constructed a golden calf and quickly forgot their God and His mighty deeds on their behalf.

Beth spoke of the deep things God had hidden which were meant for discovery and Miriam had shared with her that this was what was taught about the *Song of Songs*: that it represented the Holy of Holies—the innermost sanctuary where God dwelt in the temple; a temple that, according to Beth, was now each person who lived in Christ. Both women had agreed that even while the Chosen People had abandoned their Beloved, so, too had Christians. Neither faith had been the pure one that God so desired; and yet He continued to give opportunities for hope and repentance.

†

Miriam's attention was brought back to the present and she looked down at Joseph and once again declared her love to him, "Ani Leh'dodi Veh'dodli Li." אני לדודי ודודי לי הרעה בשושנים

And in the silence of her heart she kept the words of the *Song of Songs*.

Anah halakh Dodekh hayafah banashim anah panah Dodekh unevakshenu imakh

Dodi yarad legano laarugot habosem lirot baganim velilkot shoshanim

Ani leDodi veDodi li haroeh bashoshanim

Yafah at rayati ketirtzah navah kirushalayim ayumah kanidgalot

Hasebi einayikh minegdi shehem hirhivuni sarekh keeder haizim shegalshu min-haGilad

Shinayikh keeder harkhelim shealu min-harakhtza shekulam matimot veshakulah ein bahem

Kefelakh harimon rakatekh mibaad letzamatekh

Shishim hemah melakhot ushemonim pilagshim vaalamot ein mispar

Akhat hi yonati tamati akhat hi leimah barah hi leyoladtah rauha vanot vayeashruha melakhot ufilagshim vayehalluha

Mi-zot hanishkafah kemo-shakhar yafah khalvanah barah kakhamah ayumah kanidgalot

El-ginat egoz yaradti lirot beibei hanakhal lirot hafarkha hagefen henetzu harimonim

Lo yadati nafshi samatni markevot ami-nadiv

Shuvi shuvi hashulamit shuvi shuvi venekhezeh-bakh mah-tekhezu bashulamit kimkholat hamakhanayim

Chapter Twenty-Eight

*Too many believers do not take the battle
seriously, but beloved, there is a real war
with a real enemy seeking to devour us. He
is looking for weak, powerless people who
place their confidence in the flesh and are
naïve when it comes to the things of the
spirit.*

~ Corey Russell

Only a few days ago, Joseph had made a commitment to God. "Let me do what You want me to do and let me see what You want me to see," was what he had said. It was while he was researching St. Sharbel for the Lebanon mission that was to follow the Four Horsemen project. So he shouldn't have been surprised when the night before the Colosseum gathering he had a vision—an encounter of sorts—with the pope. Joseph wasn't quite sure what to make of it all. He had heard and read about people experiencing such things but couldn't imagine how something that miraculous could happen to him.

So, with the pope standing before him, Joseph knew that the words he had uttered from the depths of his heart had opened him to God's will in a way that he could never have imagined. Saying such things to God as wanting to do His will or wanting to "see" what God wanted you to see was, well, very different. At the time, Joseph wasn't quite sure if he believed his words would have consequences but with the appearance of the White Dove in his room now, Joseph knew that all words spoken have life within them.

The clerics were all in danger and subterfuge was underway. What would happen next was a question everyone wanted answered and Joseph was getting that answer in a very personal way.

"Blessings to you," the White Dove began.

Joseph remained silent and did his best to wrap his mind around what was happening. The pope continued, "Please do not be afraid. Do not allow your natural senses to quell your supernatural senses. You have offered your spirit to God and He has accepted your offer. In the natural realm, these unexplainable things may seem frightening and you may seek to know them in ways that are not possible.

"This is why we have fallen away from our true paths—from our true callings: we want to know the things we aren't meant to know and we ignore the things that God invites us to see. It is no different than in the Garden. Man has become his own worst enemy. He has turned his back on God and the redemption that God offers through His beloved Son.

"Now is the time for man to return to the loving arms of the Father. We are being given one more opportunity to repent—to turn away God's wrath before it is too late."

While the pope spoke these ominous words, Joseph's mind flooded with the information he had obtained while researching St. Sharbel. It did the trick; the idea of being a man in love with God filled him with peace and calm against the torrent of emotions that filled him as he listened. Clearly the man standing before him was also that sort of man: one whose life was meant to serve God and follow in the footsteps of Christ. Joseph thought of his own mother and how much she loved her faith. Her trust was always completely placed in the competent hands of Jesus. Then Joseph's mind began to absorb what was being said. The idea that man could have the power to turn back God's wrath was almost overwhelming. *What have we done?* Joseph cried out in the silence of his heart.

Joseph then smiled as if to say he understood what the pope was saying and waited for more. Which in and of itself seemed absurd. Joseph fought between wanting to discount the entire experience as a hallucination—or wishful thinking or daydreaming—and wanting it to be real. Incredibly, life-altering real. The side of him willing to suspend his natural inclination to dismiss the experience as nothing more than a trick of his mind won out and Joseph physically—visibly—relaxed as he waited for the pope to continue. *If this isn't real,* he thought to himself, *then I have nothing to lose.*

"My time in the Seat of Peter is almost over. A successor will be selected but that successor's name is yet to be known. Much depends on what happens tomorrow at the Colosseum. Aayan will be in grave danger. The hand of God is willing to be stayed but prayer, sacrifice, and repentance will be required. This was the message we were to give and it is the message that still needs to be delivered. But whether it will be or not is up to you."

Joseph wasn't quite sure what that meant and his heart raced inside his chest. *What could I possibly do to ensure that the message is delivered?* he wondered.

As if reading Joseph's mind—which didn't seem too crazy at this point—the pope went on, "My life has been ordered by God. My time on earth is almost over. Your life, too, has been ordered by God. All lives have been. It is simply up to us to enter into that relationship with Him and live in the knowledge of that truth.

"This is what the saints have done; it is what each of us is being asked to do. But nothing stands in the way of our free will. God loves us too much to take that most precious gift from us. In our freedom we are simply asked to be in obedience. Sadly, many people today think that obedience is denial of self and the things that will make us happy. And yet just the opposite is true: obedience to God brings us the most happiness for He is the one who knows us more intimately than we know ourselves. What we believe will bring us happiness or joy or peace is not always known. Unfortunately, we think that freedom to engage in what the flesh wants and desires will satisfy us; but this is not true—and our Heavenly Father knows this."

Joseph couldn't help but notice that White Dove continued to use the word "true" again and again. Joseph realized that he certainly did not know what was "true" in the way that the pope was using it; it was as if the pope had intimate knowledge of truth and wanted to share it with the world. So, too, did Aayan and Abdas and Abdeel have truth. In the end they all served God and put their own flesh to death to do so.

The pope continued unveiling truths to Joseph who was an eager student. The more the pope spoke of the things of God, the more Joseph knew what he was willing to do tomorrow—if necessary. So when Joseph entered the Colosseum the next day, his offer was complete: God was entitled to his very life and just as God offered Jesus for the lives of many, Joseph was willing to offer his life to God.

†

After the pope left—or after the vision evaporated—or after the hallucination stopped, Joseph sat in silence for more than an hour. Part of the time was simply spent trying to grasp all that the pope had revealed.

Joseph didn't even bother turning on any lights; it was now the middle of the night and yet he knew there were two phone calls he needed to make. Before doing so, he prayed; or at least he thought he prayed. At this point Joseph wasn't really sure if he really knew how to pray—and with the apparent consequences of his last time in prayer, he had to admit to himself that he was more than a bit hesitant to engage in any sort of communication with God.

Joseph knew people—many people—felt things in their spirit and he now wondered if that was what this had all been. It didn't make it less real but still he couldn't get his mind around it any other way.

Whatever it was, Joseph opened his heart to God, he thanked God for the great blessings that he had been given in his life, he implored God to protect Miriam, and he asked God for guidance and direction. Whether the pope had actually been in his room or it was simply an experience of the spirit, Joseph was being called to some sort of action that would require guidance from God.

After praying, he sat in silence. In the dark.

He wasn't sure if he was expecting some additional appearances from any number of people. He laughed to himself when he looked towards the door—*as if anyone that God would be sending would need the door!*—and waited for...Moses? Abraham? Who?

After a long time sitting in darkness and silence, and having lost all track of time, Joseph resolved to make his two phone calls. Both were to people who would not mind receiving his call day or night. The initial one was to his mother who he texted first to see if she had a few minutes to talk. She immediately replied that she had all the time in the world.

"Hi honey!" was how she answered the phone.

"Hi mom. How are you?"

"I'm good sweetheart. Everyone is doing well. How about you?' She was very good at pleasantries, allowing Joseph's reason for calling to reveal itself in its own good time. This wasn't always the case but enough calls where her anxiety made him withdraw had taught them both how to better handle their chats.

"I'm in Rome," he began. There wasn't any reason to withhold that information from her.

"How wonderful! Are you able to take in any sights?"

"Actually, I have been and plan to do a bit more before leaving."

Again she knew that if her son wanted to share what sights he had visited, he would let her know. So she waited for him to determine where the conversation was going to go from that point.

Joseph continued, "Mom, I have a couple of questions for you. A few questions about the Catholic faith. They may seem odd but I figure if anyone knows, it will be you."

His mom laughed at the other end as she had always told him that there was nothing more complex, more misunderstood, than her faith. People assumed she worshipped the mother of Christ and that many of her rituals were pagan-like. But whenever asked about this thing or that, she was always able to provide an answer that more than satisfied Joseph. He didn't always join her in her enthusiasm, but he always understood why she felt the way she did about being a follower of Jesus.

It was odd, actually, how her faith existed on two levels: intellectually and spiritually.

"Tell me a bit about experiences in the spirit...and about bi-location."

Joseph knew his mother wouldn't raise an eyebrow at the question and was glad for her open response. "Well, you know how every person is gifted in one way or another—and often people's gifts work together?"

Joseph recalled many of the books his mother had read about gifts of the Holy Spirit and had, on occasion, read excerpts himself, "Yes."

"Gifts come in many shapes and sizes." As Joseph listened to his mother, he knew that she would give him a bit of background before she specifically answered his question. Their communication improved when he became more patient with her. Since his mother was a teacher, just like Miriam's friend Beth, he now joked with her that you could take the teacher out of the classroom but couldn't take the classroom out of the teacher. With that mindset he prepared for a lesson on gifts. The fact was, it was Miriam who helped Joseph better appreciate this aspect of his conversations with his mother. Miriam had often talked about how much she had learned from Beth and while listening to her, Joseph realized how impatient he had been with his own mother whenever she took the time to explain things. He had always wanted her to get right to the point— never appreciating the time she took to give foundational information before answering his question.

His heart skipped a beat thinking that this was just one more way that he had been blessed by Miriam and then he listened as his mother continued. She talked about experiences of the spirit in which a person "knows" or has an "epiphany" or a "revelation." She talked about these experiences so matter-of-factly that Joseph believed in them, too. Reflecting upon his experience that night, he felt that God had given him a gift to "know" what the pope said and have it delivered in such a way that it became completely real.

She continued then, getting ready to move on to the topic of bi-location.

"Gifts are not things we earn. They are given to us by God. They are all—and I mean all—for God's glory and God's kingdom. St. Paul mentions these gifts and they can certainly be traced back to a few places in the Bible. In a nutshell they are being able to speak words of wisdom, words of knowledge, having great faith— almost supernatural faith—being a healer or a worker of miracles, having the gift of prophecy, being able to discern spirits, speak in tongues and interpret tongues. I would be glad to share more about those gifts whenever you want but you also wanted to know specifically about bi-location which you can see isn't one of the explicit gifts of the Holy Spirit. However, as we continue to dig we see that some people—we call them saints, Jews call them Tzadikim—are righteous people to whom God has given special gifts; but again they are always for God's kingdom and never, ever, ever for personal gain."

Joseph knew his mother was making sure that the distinction was clear as she went on, "For instance, the current president of America is said to be a 'gifted' speaker; people often call him 'charismatic.' But that is wrong from a Scriptural sense. It is using the words 'gift' and 'charism' incorrectly: not in the way we of faith use those words. America is currently voting on a law that would increase to unthinkable numbers, the amount of abortions that are performed in that country—and it would collect the money for those abortions from the citizens. Let's face it, abortion is murder. So could a man who is making sure such a law governs a country be a man using 'gifts' from God? No. Could he be 'charismatic' the way a charism is something for God's kingdom? Obviously not. Of course this is all academic since trying to change the lexicon of that country would be impossible." With that Joseph's mother snorted her derision which Joseph knew to arise from a place of complete disgust at how a country could kill so many innocent children.

"Bi-location, then, is a gift from God and very few people are given that gift during their earthly life. Imagine its power! Picture the devastation that could arise from such a gift given to someone whose heart was less than pure.

"Padre Pio is probably the most well-known person to have had this unique—and misunderstood—gift. Certainly anyone hearing about him who was not a believer would simply dismiss it as foolishness or even evil; but you have to look at the way that Padre Pio used the gift before making that kind of determination.

"Compare it to the way the President of the United States uses his so-called 'gifts.' He supports the killing of babies. Now consider how Padre Pio used his gifts. Let me just grab my book so I can be sure of the facts."

Joseph heard his mother put down the phone and walk out of the room. He knew the room well. As her feet padded across the floor, Joseph could see the beautiful tapestry rug that had been given to them by his grandparents. It was truly a work of art. The rich bold colors of reds and golds woven throughout creating a mosaic of flowers and urns amid a border of vines. Joseph longed to walk across it himself, just one more time. He thought of all the games he and his sisters played while sprawled across its warm nap. Joseph could see the large, ornate cabinet with its glass doors. Tucked safely behind the doors, but for all to see, were the treasures of his family: small cups from which his parents drank their dark, aromatic coffee; stacks of mismatched but equally loved plates that ranged in size and color were the remnants of sets from both his mother and his father's grandparents and great-grandparents; and at the center of it all sat a framed picture of the three children—Joseph, Sarah, and Sipporah—when they were quite young. Joseph remembered well the day the picture was taken. His parents were eagerly anticipating the arrival of their parents. It was a rare occasion when the entire family would be together. The acceptance of Joseph's father to a prestigious position had been the circumstance which they would all be celebrating. The three children were dressed in their best outfits and each was quite excited to have both sets of grandparents at their beck and call.

It was difficult to keep the kids still for the picture but in the end, one was snapped which had taken a bit of bribing. Afterwards, the entire family enjoyed an ice-cream sundae—as promised by the bribe that got them all to stand still for what ultimately became the favorite picture for Marcy and Benjamin Klein—Joseph's parents. In fact, the grandparents had also requested copies and those had just as prominent a spot in their homes as it did in the Klein home; so whenever the grandchildren visited, they were always reminded of that special day.

Joseph was wrangled out of his reminiscing when he heard his mother's footsteps approach the phone. "Here it is," she declared with triumph. "Are you there?" she asked before beginning with some of the facts she wanted to share about Padre Pio.

"Yes, and thank you so much, mom, for helping me out with this."

"You know I could do this for hours so maybe I should be thanking you!" she replied—and he knew it to be true. He had often watched as his mother would get so engrossed in a book about this saint or that pope or explanations of some particular practice that if anyone walked in the room and said "Hi!" she would about jump out of her skin, so transported would she be by the words on the page.

Whoever it was who had caused her to jump would laugh and say something like "It's just me, remember me? I live here, too, so it shouldn't be a surprise!" This always made his mother laugh—at her own foibles and at the easy way her kids could tease her.

She began explaining about Pio's supposed bi-location abilities and Joseph listened intently—his own reasons still withheld from her. "The first thing he seems to want to make clear whenever he speaks about this gift is that it is only used when there is a grave danger or some soul is in jeopardy."

Joseph's spine tingled hearing those words. He wanted to know, "Does he give examples?"

"Not really. Maybe that is something that he knew and for him it didn't need explanation. That sort of thing happens a lot in Scripture—the writer simply assumes a certain experience or knowledge of the reader and goes from there. Take, for instance, the word 'remember' in Mass when the bread and wine are actually changed into the body and blood of Christ. Most people nowadays don't understand what Jesus meant when He said, 'Do this in memory of me,' and so they think this entire act is just symbolic of something; but if they knew what the Scripture writers knew and everyone knew at the time, they would understand that 'remember' actually means to the Jewish mind to 'make present.' So when God had given the Chosen People instructions to 'remember' Exodus through their Passover Seder, He was actually instructing them to, each year, become present in it! Time and space were being suspended and they weren't 'remembering' in the sense that we think of the word—recalling something— they were, through God's grace and under His instructions, making the Passover dinner present. They were being part of it! This is exactly what happens during Mass. We aren't 'remembering' in a symbolic way, we are participating in a real and anointed way!"

Joseph could hear his mother's voice jump all over as if she had just experienced an epiphany, although he knew she had understood transubstantiation long before this phone call.

"But I digress…"

Joseph laughed and agreed, "Yes, you do!"

"However, my point is still valid: Padre Pio probably understood what it meant for someone to be in 'grave danger' and did not need to elaborate."

"Point taken," was all Joseph said in response and to encourage his mom to continue. He was so grateful that Miriam had helped him have patience with his mother and her explanations. When he was honest with himself, he could admit that he had shown his mother—just a few short years ago—quite a lot of disrespect and impatience when she tried to share her passion and enthusiasm with him.

"So, it looks like most of his bi-location experiences happened in the early to mid 1950s." Marcy shared some of the bi-location accounts of Padre Pio and also the stories of his stigmata—receiving the wounds of Christ. "It also looks like some of the bi-locations occurred during wartime. Others happened in odd situations like a car just about crashing and Pio intervening while, according to everyone interviewed, he was actually in the convent. It seems like there are a variety of instances and corroborated accounts of his bi-location that it was a true gift."

As his mother concluded, Joseph wasn't sure he felt convinced and if it weren't for his time with the pope, he may not even have been slightly swayed by what she just shared. "Okay, thanks mom."

"Oh! Here, Padre Pio's body was exhumed in 2008, some 40 years after his death, and is now visited by thousands of pilgrims a day. Apparently it is incorrupt. You know, completely preserved."

That added a bit more credibility to the Padre Pio story but Joseph still had his reservations. "Interesting," was all he added before giving his mother his love and making his second phone call.

†

While Joseph was making inquiries to his mother and his close friend, Miriam slept fitfully—if at all. She dreamt of her mother but it wasn't like any dream she had ever experienced. In it, Ayala came to her and reached out a hand towards Miriam. Miriam was a young girl of maybe fourteen or fifteen and Ayala was likewise a younger mother.

"Miriam," her mother began and Miriam looked up into her mother's eyes which were so vibrant and full of love that Miriam almost could not maintain her gaze.

"There is so much for a mother to tell a daughter. There is so much for a parent to tell a child. If I could invite you into my heart you would know all the things I wish to share with you and you would find in them great peace and joy. This is because there is no greater love than what a parent has for a child. But you are not just my daughter; you are a beloved daughter of the Most High God. I have been given the extreme honor and privilege to know you in this earthly life—to walk with you on your journey."

Miriam could see tears well up in her mother's eyes and did not quite understand. As if reading her mind, her mother said, "You cannot imagine how deep my love is for you and I know that; but it does not change it. Just as you cannot know the love Hashem has for you does not change it, either. But love does not always protect us from the evil of the world. It does, however, give us a place of refuge. You are destined to experience great sadness in your life but I want you to remember how much you are loved. You are a woman of great character and courage. You are a shining star whose light will be a light to others. Light the Sabbath candle of your heart, Miriam.

"Do not be afraid of the path that Adonai has put before you. Trust in God as He loves you more than I do. I understand that now. While I never imagined that there could be a greater love for you than I have, I am able to see that my love for you pales in comparison to the love that the God of Abraham, Isaac, Jacob, and Joseph has for you! It makes my heart sing to know this!"

The joy in Ayala's voice carried Miriam to a place of great love and peace. She was deep in her sleep and did not wish to wake up; she did not want to let go of her mother's hand—literally or figuratively. In it she found the safety that she longed for while the emptiness that often welled up inside her chest was gone. But her mother cajoled her into rising, "You must wake up, my sweet daughter, these words of mine must live in your conscious mind. They must find a home in your heart."

With that, Miriam's eyes opened—against the inclination of every fiber of her being. They darted around the dark room. Miriam held her breath and waited for her heart to stop pounding so violently in her chest. She whispered into the darkness, "I love you Emma. Please don't leave me again."

†

Joseph's next call was to his good friend, Shemuel. Most of their friends called him by his more common name: Samuel. Some even called him 'Sammy,' but Joseph had always preferred the sound of his Hebrew name: Shemuel. It was probably because the first time Joseph saw Shemuel write it in Hebrew—שְׁמוּאֵל—Joseph felt as if the letters on the page spoke to him. Shemuel went on to explain how Hebrew letters did have a life of their own and were considered the building blocks of creation. Shemuel then taught a willing student the letters of the Hebrew alphabet before giving him what Joseph felt to be incredible insight. Shemuel explained that the first letter of the Torah is the letter 'Bet' ב and the last letter is a 'Lamed' ל; together they create the word 'lev' לָב which is heart or love. In its entirety, the *Torah* reveals God's love to His people!

Shemuel was a rather short young man with a head full of thick, unruly, jet-black hair. He always seemed just one week overdue for a haircut which meant that his dark hair tended to have a life of his own. Whenever Shemuel spoke of something that excited him, his head bobbed all over and it took great concentration on the listener's behalf to hear what Shemuel was saying instead of watching his spot-on, albeit unintentional, bobble-head imitation. This time was no different as Shemuel went on explaining some things to Joseph about the *Torah*—or what was also called the *Pentateuch*, the first five books of Scripture.

"Before God took Moses from this life, He told Moses that He wanted to leave His people with a token of His love. Maybe God felt a bit bad since they had been chastised and punished a lot. Theirs had really been a difficult existence. Whatever the reason, God dictated to Moses everything that He wanted His people to know and Moses wrote the *Torah*. That is why the Jewish people are called the 'People of the Book.' They are bound to God through those words and learn of His great love for them from *Torah*. Every year the Scroll is read—from beginning to end—as a reminder of God's love and how they have a special place in His heart. Some Catholic saint captured this odd relationship between God and those he loved. Odd because you'd think if God was crazy in love with you, you'd have a pretty care-free existence. But in this instance that was definitely not the case. Anyhow, I'm not quite sure who it was but some saint said something like this to God, 'If this is how you treat your friends, it is no surprise you have so few—or any!'"

Joseph's response seemed a bit juvenile at the time but he did feel rather in awe of what Shemuel was saying about the *Torah* being words of love. Joseph recalled how his mother spoke of Jesus, a Jewish man who was also known as the 'Word Made Flesh.' A coincidence like that couldn't be taken lightly. So the *Torah* was about God's love and then Jesus was an incarnate, visible, tangible, touchable, man who embodied that love. God took the words from the pages and gave them flesh. Jesus came into the world. "Wow!" was all he could muster to encompass the epiphany exploding in his mind and heart.

It was for Joseph a turning point.

Shemuel just smiled his friendly smile and agreed, "Yeah, I know! Wow, right?"

Shemuel picked up the other end of the phone just as Joseph was smiling at the memory of this exchange which had transported Joseph back as if it were taking place right at that very moment.

"Joseph! I was just thinking about you! How weird, right? I was thinking about the time I taught you the Hebrew alphabet and some stuff about the *Torah*. Weird coincidence. So how are you? I haven't talked with you in ages. How's that sweetheart Miriam? Have you told her yet how much she means to you?"

At this point, nothing seemed too bizarre to Joseph. He wanted to say, "Welcome to my world," but instead said, "Yes and no. I've told her and yet I haven't been incredibly specific. I have, however, spoken with her father and her brother about my intentions. I've also shipped them something that I will give her when we get back to Israel. But enough about me. How about you? How's my 'End-Times' friend doing?"

Joseph had begun calling Shemuel his 'End-Times' friend a few years ago when Shemuel's passing interest in reading end-time prophecies rapidly grew into a full-blown obsession. Shemuel put his razor-sharp intellect into collecting every end-time prophecy ever written and was conducting a mammoth research project that was, just like Joseph's current and future missions, part political and part religious. Everywhere Joseph turned, the two aspects of life were merging.

"Busy. I'm very busy. I'm also getting very religious—or spiritual, I'm not really sure what the correct word would be to describe how I feel. Let's just say that the more I learn, the more I believe. Quite the opposite of what I expected. But if you share that with anyone I will completely deny that I said it. I have a reputation to uphold."

"I suppose I'm going through the same thing," was Joseph's honest response which sounded more like him talking to himself than him answering his friend. "Then you are probably just the person who can help me," he went on, more resolutely.

"Sure! What's up? You sound a bit distant. And I don't mean physically distant; I mean you sound emotionally distant. Something on your mind, friend?"

Joseph could always count on Shemuel to cut to the chase. It was a characteristic that many found abrasive but Joseph found refreshing. "Well," Joseph said, "I'll preface this with an oath of confidentiality. Just like I've given one for your disclaimer about becoming more religious or spiritual."

Both men laughed and Shemuel assured Joseph that this conversation was no different than any other they had ever had. It was always in confidence.

Encouraged, Joseph went on to share with his friend the events that had transpired in the past few days while in Rome. To the degree needed, Joseph also shared the essential nature of the Four Horsemen mission—and what would be taking place the next day. When he was done speaking he heard Shemuel release a slow, long whistle at the other end of the phone. Joseph waited for Shemuel to process what he had just heard. Joseph knew enough about his pal—and was comfortable enough in their friendship—to let silence sit between them.

"I'm going to fax over a few documents to you. All this fits in with what I've been researching but I think that a couple of things specifically speak to what is happening right now. These are things that have been portended by many prophets over the ages. If you would have shared this with me just two years ago I would have suggested a strong drink and a vacation; but now I'm suggesting prayer and fasting. These are the things that will stay the hand of God. Those—and selfless acts of love."

Of all the things that Joseph imagined Shemuel saying, these were the last things he wanted to hear. The reality was that Shemuel was Joseph's last hope that all he really did need was a strong drink and a vacation. Maybe Joseph knew the truth but still he had held out vestiges of hope that this last phone call would prove Joseph incorrect. But, alas, that was not to be the case.

Shemuel continued, "A few prophecies really stand out that I want to share based upon what you've just said."

"Okay, I'm all ears," was Joseph's permission for his good friend to finish opening the can of worms, the Pandora's box.

"St. Francis of Paola was born in Italy in the 15th century. He prophesied about a man he called the 'Great Monarch' who would lead the world to a new and holy time. I share this first because at the heart of prophecy should always be a chance for repentance and hope. For the most part, unless it was really far too late—as in the time of Noah—God gives people a chance to change their ways, to turn back to Him and not turn their backs on Him. But even during Noah's time, consider how long it took for him to build the ark. All the while people could have been paying attention and changing their ways; but instead they ridiculed Noah. I guess you could say that we live in a time where an ark is being built but, again, no one is paying attention—or they are ridiculing the craftsmen who are building it.

"The ridicule doesn't stop the builder even though it may make the building of it more difficult."

Shemuel chuckled and said, "I think I'm enjoying this ark metaphor a bit too much but you get what I'm saying."

"I do," said Joseph, also chuckling.

"So while St. Francis of Paola talks about this 'Great Monarch' he also prophesizes about the evil that God will permit against His church. A lot of what he says seems to be applicable today."

Shemuel anticipated Joseph's rebuttal that all people felt that they lived in the end-times by quickly saying, "Before you stop me, please read through what I will be faxing to you. You will see that too many of the prophecies line up for our current time to be able to dismiss them. I know that I no longer am able to just ignore them as if they were irrelevant.

"What seems particularly germane from the St. Francis of Paola prophecies—and why I bring them up to you now—is that they predict that many bishops, prelates, and priests will 'fall asleep' and that Rome will suffer the consequences. Things will be destroyed, the city will be brought to ruin. During this time, according to the prophet, Christians will be ridiculed and there will be a high regard for 'knowledge' while morals and the truths of the faith will be held up to derision, censure, and criticism. This will all happen during the time that St. Francis of Paola calls the 'Fifth Period.'

"I think another one that can't be ignored comes from Mary of Agreda. She lived during the 17th century and speaks of the very special role Mary, the Mother of Christ, will have in salvation. You may not know this, Joseph, but there have been many apparitions of Mary over the past couple of centuries. All of this seems to confirm what Mary of Agreda said: that Mary, the Mother of Christ, will lead many to her Son. You see Joseph, that is why she keeps appearing: she wants to convert as many souls as possible for her Son. I've come to see it this way: she watched her Son die a horrific death, this baby that she bore grew into a man who died for all; how, then, could she not do everything in her power to help people choose Him? No one would want this more than she does. Any mother would understand and agree."

Joseph grunted and Shemuel stopped speaking long enough to allow him to accept and process some of the knowledge that was coming at him at lightning speed. At one point, not too long ago, Shemuel would have called it theory—or conjecture—but he no longer believed that it was just speculation. The more he researched, the more convinced Shemuel became that these were the times prophesied about during which each person was given a last chance, so to speak, to make a choice for God. Shemuel began telling friends and family: buckle in; it's going to be a bumpy ride.

After a few minutes, Shemuel continued, "Volumes have been written about one of these apparitions: Fatima. Fatima is in Portugal which was evangelized by James. A few centuries after, it was invaded by Muslim Moors. According to a variety of sources, the Blessed Virgin Mary interceded for the Portuguese and they eventually became independent. This was early in the 12th century. A couple of centuries later, Spain attempted to conquer Portugal. Again, credit is given to Mary for her intercession and in gratitude, King John I built a magnificent monastery: the Royal Convent of Saint Mary of Victory in the Battle. You can no doubt see that these incidents play an important part in Portuguese history and are certainly at the heart of their great devotion to the Blessed Mother. I think that is important to mention because it either gives more credibility—or less—to what eventually happens with the children to whom Mary appears. Personally, I would have preferred the visions come to non-believers but then I wonder if that would really be advantageous. Like when the Resurrected Christ appeared to Mary Magdalene; she already believed in Him. Why not appear to someone who didn't believe? But then would they have dismissed it as a hallucination? Then I think to myself: who am I to question God's methods?"

Joseph was, himself, in the middle of doing just that: questioning God's methods. So Shemuel's words felt as if they were spoken directly from God to Joseph via Shemuel. Joseph was physically startled by them and paced around the room while he continued to listen.

"So this becomes the backdrop of what happens in this small village very early 20th century. Pretty much we're talking about dirt poor, simple people who practiced their faith in humble, devout ways."

Joseph's mind was immediately filled with St. Sharbel and he interjected, "Yes, I can picture it."

Shemuel continued, "People nowadays can't imagine such an existence—no 'things,' just a simple life often lived on the very edge of poverty but yet somehow filled with joy and hope. They—these people who many would call 'poor'—were really very rich. They totally got that this existence—this fleeting, meager time on earth—wasn't the one that mattered. Their eyes were on heaven and their eternal existence with God.

"I don't want to do a disservice but will give you a brief summary of Fatima. The first apparition was in early 1916. An angel appeared to three young children—they were around ten years old give or take. There were two girls and a boy. One of the girls and the boy were brother and sister. Anyhow, the angel appears to them while they are tending sheep or having just finished and are playing, and the first thing the angel says is that they shouldn't be afraid. Now let me remind you that those are important words. Remember that Gabriel told Mary not to be afraid when he shared with her that she had 'found favor with God.' And then there was an angel who told the shepherds about the birth of Jesus that they shouldn't be afraid."

Joseph interjected that he understood the weight of those words as he remembered the first words the pope spoke to him just a few hours ago, "Do not be afraid."

"So the first thing this angel says to the kids is that they shouldn't be afraid. He then teaches them what has become known as the 'Pardon Prayer.' It is a prayer these kids would say for hours on end."

Joseph heard a few pages being sifted through and then Shemuel said, "Here are the exact words: 'My God, I believe, I adore, I hope and I love You! I ask pardon of You for those who do not believe, do not adore, do not hope and do not love You!' So before these kids are visited by Mary, they are visited a few times by this angel who sort of sets the stage. That just makes a lot of sense to me—not that God needs my approval! But think, as an example, of how David was prepared for his role against Goliath by being a shepherd and fighting off wild beasts and protecting his flock. No one was paying attention to this scrawny kid but God was giving him opportunities to prepare. It makes me ask the burning question: What are we being prepared for right now?

"Anyhow, about a year later, in 1917, was Mary's first apparition to the kids—they had been prepared and were now ready. Just like the angel, Mary's first concern was to make sure the children weren't afraid. After that, Mary's question to the children was to see if they would be willing to bear sufferings as reparation for sins. Think about that! Here are some very young kids who are asked if they would be willing to accept and offer up suffering for others? They consented—which honestly floors me! I have to admit that I don't know any young kids who would be willing to do such a thing—or would even know what it all meant. Or maybe the young really are examples of the sort of innocence we are supposed to emulate. Who knows?"

Shemuel became uncharacteristically quiet as he contemplated his own question. Joseph gave him the time to do so and simply sat in silence on the other end of the phone. There was a serene feeling that was enveloping him and for the first time in many days he was not a sea of emotions; rather, he was calm and without any agitation.

Shemuel finished his silent, personal reflection and continued, "There is so much to this—too much almost—and I am going to write down the names of a couple of books I recommend you read. Overall, though, Mary's apparitions are about repentance and turning to her Son. They are about prayer and fasting and offering up everything—just as the angel had previously told them.

"Oh, one more thing I need to mention. Throughout all these prophecies seems to run a theme about three days of darkness. Now just like the angel appeared to the children before the appearance of Mary—and just like God gave a number of plagues to convince Pharaoh before the really big one—so, too, will there be signs before the three days of darkness. Many of these things—these signs—can be said to have existed at any point in time but I think it would be foolish to ignore their rampant prevalence now. For instance, the disintegration of family life and moral order. The Sodom-and-Gomorrah lifestyle as I have come to call it will be the way of the land. I think if you just look at what is happening across all countries you will see how there is no longer any inclination to overcome carnal desires. Just look at what has happened within the Catholic Church! And it doesn't get any better anywhere else. Everyone has succumbed to their lustful proclivities of the flesh and ego."

Joseph listened and thought of the Four Horsemen as true remnants of what was left of God's will on the earth. These men were being called to physical martyrdom as surely as they were being called to speak out in these dark times. He grunted in agreement as Shemuel continued.

"So these three days of darkness will have forewarnings but most will be blind—or choose to believe in themselves and the rule of the land over God. But these will be the last moments of choice. I can't help but see the similarities between these prophecies and what happened in Egypt with Moses and Pharaoh. We learn our best lessons when we learn from history.

"Anyhow, once we are in these three days of darkness, there are certain things we can do—again I see those as reminiscent of what God asked the People of the Book to do when He instructed them to cover their doorposts with lamb's blood. We, too, will be asked to do things like have blessed candles as our only source of light and keep our doors and windows locked and avoid looking out into the world as this will cause our immediate death, Lot's-wife style. Not necessarily a pillar of salt; but immediate, nonetheless."

"We?" Joseph quickly interjected.

"Yes," admitted Shemuel, "I say 'we' because I am in that camp that believe. I have blessed candles and holy water and some food and blankets. I cannot look back into history and then choose to ignore lessons I was astounded that people during the times chose to ignore. I don't know if any of this is helping you at all…"

"It is exactly what I was hoping for in regards to getting a few odd things straightened out. Now let me ask you this: do you think that it is too late to turn things around? You've said we live in a time where people have to make choices. Will they? And if they will—and do—will it be enough? You've said you are prepared so does that mean we should all be prepared and just accept it as inevitable?"

Shemuel thought about this for a moment. "I'm not sure. I wish I were, but I'm not. I can tell you what I am sure of, though. I am positive that if we don't make the effort to try and change we *will* see the end. So then why wouldn't we make the effort? The whole thing reminds me of a fable which didn't make sense at the time but definitely does now. Have you ever heard the story about the pious Jewish man who rode a mule into town and when he arrived at his destination there was a rabbi at the door? The man asked the rabbi this question: 'Teacher, should I tie my mule up or trust that God will keep him here for me.' The rabbi responded: 'Tie him up; but trust in God.' I think that best explains how our reactions ought to be right now: prepare but trust."

Joseph laughed and said that, actually, he had heard that story. He also understood that hearing it again was God's way of making sure he got its important message.

Shemuel then continued, "Here, let me read this that the angel told those kids at Fatima. I think it really continues to sum up how we ought to be living right now. He said to them: 'Make of everything you can a sacrifice, and offer it to God as an act of reparation for the sins by which He is offended, and in supplication for the conversion of sinners.'

"That's what I do know—that we need to make the conscious decision to turn away from the world's way of doing and seeing things to God's way. We fast and pray for the best while we prepare for the worst—all the while trusting in God."

Joseph thanked Shemuel for his time and insights and hung up promising to keep in touch. The calm that descended upon him remained with him as he knew in his heart what he had to offer up the next day—which was already making its presence known in the sunrise—at the Colosseum. It seemed to come down to one thing: sacrifice.

Just as Joseph's mind accepted what his heart knew, the fax machine began offering papers. They quietly piled up and Joseph walked over to the tray and pulled one off to read. In Shemuel's own writing was written:

> *This is another prayer the angel taught the kids at Fatima...*
>
> *Most Holy Trinity, Father, Son and Holy Spirit, I adore You profoundly, and I offer You the most precious Body, Blood, Soul, and Divinity of Jesus Christ, present in all the tabernacles of the world, in reparation for the outrages, sacrileges and indifference with which He Himself is offended. And through the infinite merits of His most Sacred Heart, and the Immaculate Heart of Mary, I beg of You the conversion of poor sinners...*
>
> *amazing, huh?*

"Amazing, indeed," Joseph said as the sun continued rising and his room began filling with the light of the day. Shuffling through the papers, one caught his eye. His mother had apparently sent it through while Shemuel's papers were making their way into the tray and it now begged to be read. At the top of the page she had written a short note:

> *This is the prayer that I often say to begin my day. You may find it consoling. I love you, sweetheart. Mom.*

The typed heading identified it as the *Lorica of St. Patrick.* Joseph stood facing the window from where he could see the beautiful sunrise and read it out loud.

> *I arise today through a mighty strength, the invocation of the Trinity, through belief in the Threeness, through confession of the Oneness of the Creator of creation.*

> *I arise today through the strength of Christ with His Baptism, through the strength of His Crucifixion with His Burial, through the strength of His Resurrection with His Ascension, through the strength of His descent for the Judgment of Doom.*

Joseph continued reading even though his vision was blurred from the tears in his eyes. As he came to the end he found himself choking back sobs as the words were more real than he could have imagined:

> *Christ with me, Christ before me, Christ behind me, Christ in me, Christ beneath me, Christ above me, Christ on my right, Christ on my left, Christ in breadth, Christ in length, Christ in height, Christ in the heart of every man who thinks of me, Christ in the mouth of every man who speaks of me, Christ in every eye that sees me, Christ in every ear that hears me.*

> *I arise today through a mighty strength, the invocation of the Trinity, through belief in the Threeness, through confession of the Oneness of the Creator of creation.*

Salvation is of the Lord. Salvation is of the Lord. Salvation is of Christ. May Thy Salvation, O Lord, be ever with us.

When Joseph finished reading the prayer, He splashed water on his face, changed his shirt and squared his shoulders as he walked out the door.

He made a note to himself that he would have to study up on St. Patrick.

He then laughed when he thought how very clever his mother was in faxing over the prayer and keeping him on the hook. She absolutely knew he wouldn't leave it alone and would delve further into studying the saints.

Chapter Twenty-Nine

He said, "It is finished."

~John 19:30b

Luke and Elizabeth made it out of the Colosseum safely. The streets of Rome were in complete chaos. People were running and screaming. Beth heard the distinct sounds of sirens coming from all directions and yet knew that none of the Polizia di Stato would be able to make it through the throngs of people and deliver the aid that so many needed. Luke's sheer determination moved them towards their building. His vise-like grip on her hand made it go numb and yet she did not complain. She stayed in tow with Luke agilely moving through the crowds. At one point he bent down to help lift an older man off the street. But even when he did this, Luke would not let go of Beth. This made it difficult for Luke to offer assistance but he did so nonetheless. Once the older man had been safely ensconced in a doorway, they continued another few meters before arriving at their destination. Beth could almost hear Luke's thoughts: *What in God's name have I gotten us into?*

Elizabeth's mind then reeled as it went back to the day that Ayala died in the bombing in Israel. *Could this really be happening again?* was all she kept thinking to herself.

Luke opened the door with the key, still holding onto Beth as if she would surely be pulled into the raging tide of people and swept away. Once inside the building they nearly crawled up the stairs to the apartment. Fumbling now with the keys and lock, the day seemed to overtake Luke. Beth gently removed the keys from his hand and inserted the correct one into the knob. She heard the click and felt Luke hold her arm while he opened the door. With incredible love he guided her in towards safety and bolted the door shut. Although the windows were closed they could still hear the screaming voices and the sirens. Luke and Beth didn't say a word to each other but walked slowly towards the window where each peered out into the streets. Beth made the sign of the cross and began saying the *Lord's Prayer*. Luke joined her with words that trembled. Their strength existed separately from one another's weaknesses. It was a by-product of a life built together. Luke understood that now in a way that he had never before understood in their marriage. It became something palpable and strong, able to withstand that which came against it once they made the decision to honor it and exist within it with one another.

Luke began to cry. He cried out of sadness and he cried out of joy. He thought of his sins which sat heavy on his heart and he recognized with new eyes the way God had blessed him through his family. There was no embarrassment or shame in Luke's tears, they simply, slowly made their way down his face and dropped onto the floor. If possible, they seemed cleansing. It was as if he had never seen his life through the eyes of Christ and now that he did, the view filled him with emotions that were tied to all the events of his life as if they were happening again—but with a new purpose: to bind Luke to God. Luke understood that being yoked to God wasn't about bondage but about freedom and Luke yearned for that freedom. He desired it unlike anything he had ever desired or sought. All the goals of his career paled in comparison to this new goal that sat before him: to live out the rest of his days seeking God's will for his life.

Beth knelt on the floor next to him and put her hand on his shoulder. He faced her and she looked deep into his eyes. She did not want to say a word; she needed to know that they were truly one and that her thoughts were at that very moment also his thoughts. She wanted to believe that the love she felt for him was so real that words would only dilute it—that simply being next to him was enough.

After a few moments, Beth reached over to the end table and picked up a booklet that she had found tucked into a drawer in the bedroom dresser. It was filled with prayers to the Sacred Heart and one in particular had previously caught her attention. She felt she needed to read it. It was called *the Act of Reparation to the Sacred Heart.*

With Luke at her side, she quietly began reading from the page.

> *Most sweet Jesus, whose overflowing charity for men is requited by so much forgetfulness, negligence and contempt, behold us prostrate before Thy altar eager to repair by a special act of homage the cruel indifference and injuries, to which Thy loving Heart is everywhere subject...*

After she finished the entire prayer, Luke lifted the pamphlet from her hands and leafed through the few pages until he came upon the *Litany of the Most Sacred Heart of Jesus.* He led and Beth responded as directed.

> *Lord, have mercy on us.*
> *Christ, have mercy on us.*
> *Lord, have mercy on us.*
> *Christ, hear us.*
> *Christ, graciously hear us.*
> *God, the Father of heaven, have mercy on us.*
> *God the Son, Redeemer of the World, have mercy on us.*

God the Holy Ghost, have mercy on us.
Holy Trinity, one God, have mercy on us.

Luke continued reading to the end…

Lamb of God, who takes away the sins of the world,
spare us, O Lord.
Lamb of God, who takes away the sins of the world,
graciously hear us, O Lord .
Lamb of God, who takes away the sins of the world,
have mercy on us.

Chapter Thirty

When we are in daily contact with our
Savior, we become ever more sensitive to
what pleases or displeases him.

~ Edith Stein

Covered in bloody clothes, Miriam made her way out of the Colosseum. The ambulanza and the medical team tried but failed to save Joseph's life. He had died in her arms hearing her words of love. Now she walked aimlessly through the streets being jostled by the crowds which were pushing their way towards safety within their homes, apartments, and hotels.

Miriam's Mossad training had failed her in every way. She could not save Joseph's life nor could she get control of the chaotic situation taking place around her. She walked helplessly as thousands of people scrambled across the stone steps of the Colosseum, pushing and shoving past one another with little care as to one another's safety. Miriam heard many people scream when they had noticed Joseph's bloody body in the center arena but not one person ran towards him—or her—to help. Instead, the site was impetus for them to all flee in the opposite direction.

Miriam knew from her own experience that self-preservation was rearing its ugly head. She did not fault those who fled; however, her heart ached with the realization that her beloved Joseph had offered his life for them and they had little or no sense of that sacrifice made on their behalf.

The ambulanza driver did not allow her to accompany Joseph's body to the hospital so Miriam stood, alone and lonely, and watched as the vehicle drove away. The other agents had taken their charges to safety but Miriam could not manage enough energy to care. She knew that the mission would go on without her and Joseph—as it should—and now she simply wanted to seek comfort and refuge somewhere, someplace.

As she stumbled along the streets, she remembered seeing Beth and Luke on a balcony in a building not far from where she now stood. Determination took hold of her and she straightened her shoulders and walked to the vicinity where she had seen her American friend. Miriam closed her eyes and let her training take over. She brought to her mind the building, the balcony, and the windows. It was only a matter of minutes before she knew exactly where to find Elizabeth. Miriam then took the first step towards the consolation and protection she knew she would find in that companionship.

Walking up to the set of buttons that flanked the door, Miriam pushed the buzzer for the apartment that she knew would be Elizabeth's. She waited a moment before depressing the buzzer a second time. Somehow Miriam knew that Elizabeth would be there and Miriam found herself thanking God for the happenstance of having seen Beth and thus providing a safe haven in this, Miriam's desperate time of need.

Miriam heard a clicking sound and knew that either Beth or her husband were opening up the intercom but whoever it was had been unwilling to speak. She took her cue and said, "Beth? Luke? This is Miriam. Miriam Goldfarb. May I come in?"

"Oh my gosh! Miriam!" was all Miriam heard as the buzzer was held long and hard to allow Miriam's access to the building. Once inside, Miriam was overcome with exhaustion and was unsure if her legs would take to up the stairs. She heard someone rapidly descending the steps and was relieved to see Luke's strong presence.

He gasped when he saw Miriam and immediately asked, "Are you hurt? Do we need to get you to a hospital?" Sincere concern laced the alarm in his voice. Obviously he and Beth had been able to leave the Colosseum before witnessing what had happened to Joseph.

"I am unharmed," was Miriam's response but even the words sounded shallow and untrue to her. Her mind dared her to define 'unharmed.'

Luke wrapped his right arm around Miriam's waist and she looped her left arm around his neck which provided the support she needed to walk up the staircase; her full weight leaned against Luke while Joseph's blood made its way onto the side of Luke's shirt.

As the pair wound their way up the stairs they could hear Beth, obviously standing at the doorway holding the apartment door open, quietly calling out, "Is everything okay?"

Luke dared not answer and prayed that the silence would not add to Beth's growing concern. In a moment Luke and Miriam rounded the corner and into Beth's line of vision. Her gasp said it all. Both Luke and Miriam were now covered in blood and for a moment Luke thought that Beth might faint. Her face immediately lost all of its color and as her legs gave way she slumped against the doorpost. Only through the grace of God did she not crumble onto the floor but, instead, stood erect—as if a soldier at attention.

Luke knew that "mother-mode" had kicked in—and he was quite relieved. He had seen it many times over their life together. Once, when one of the boys had fallen out of a tree, Beth was forced to contend with blood and bone sticking through flesh. Like those miraculous feats where a grandmother lifts a car off a toddler, in a nanosecond Beth went from pale white to "in-charge" wherein she calmly gave orders to Sophia to watch her younger brother while Beth maneuvered the other into the car for a ride to the hospital.

"Mother-mode." Luke remembered it well during times of stomach flu and bad report cards. It made itself known through tears and through childhood tragedies that included the pain caused by lost friendships and the death of pets.

"Mother-mode." It seemed appropriate that it kicked in now as Luke recalled the deep fondness Elizabeth held for Miriam—and all of Miriam's family for that matter. Indeed, the tea set that they had sent her when she had returned home from her pilgrimage was something that Beth cherished. It was a tangible reminder of the people God had brought into her life— and now wasn't the time to let one of these precious souls suffer.

"Luke, take her to the couch. I will get some warm water and the first aid kit—just in case." Beth could see that the blood was not oozing from any wound on either Miriam or Luke and quickly concluded that it was from someone else.

Miriam's smile showed her appreciation even while her mouth was unable to find any words. She was losing consciousness and her head rolled back as Luke gently placed her upon the sofa. Beth's mother-mode continued as she instructed Luke to change and allow her some privacy with Miriam. Beth quickly ran into the bedroom before Luke left Miriam's side so that she could grab a clean outfit. With a pair of casual knit pants and a loose knit top in hand, Beth returned and Luke left the two women alone. He went to the bathroom to wash up but not before grabbing clean clothes as well.

Beth took a cloth soaked in warm, sudsy water and gently washed Miriam's hands and face. The sink was just a few steps from the couch but still she hesitated to leave Miriam's side to fetch clean water. She continued to rinse the rag and wash Miriam until it became obvious that the water in the bowl was too blood-soaked to be of use and Beth was forced to get fresh water. As she stood at the sink and rinsed the bowl out and filled it with clean water she watched as Miriam moved her head from side to side. Beth could see tears streaming down Miriam's face and was immediately back at her side. Slowly, Beth removed Miriam's blouse and replaced it with the clean one. She did the same with the pants. Beth was overcome with the memories of doing the same for herself when she had been struck by shards of glass from the bomb that took Ayala's life. The sheer memory of that day forced Beth to be strong. She resolved that she would be strong for Ayala's daughter. This gave her physical and emotional strength that welled up from within and became a force from which she knew she would draw over the next few minutes and even days.

Miriam spoke quietly, "Toda."

"You are very welcome, dear friend." In the movies the victim or heroine was always told to save their strength but Beth wasn't about to say such things to Miriam. Strength would come in the form of the words that Miriam would undoubtedly need to express and share. Strength would come from knowing that agape love existed between the two friends and that Miriam was not alone.

"Joseph has died," was Miriam's simple sentence.

In the letters that had been exchanged over the years since Elizabeth's pilgrimage to the Holy Land, Beth knew that Joseph was another Mossad agent with whom Miriam worked. Beth could also very easily read between the lines and see that he was someone that had gone from friend to love interest—even if Miriam had not seen it. Beth expressed her thoughts to Miriam in so many words and knew that Miriam was quite close to recognizing the truth.

Beth remembered the words of comfort she had been taught by a neighbor of the Goldfarb's when she had prepared to attend Shivah for Ayala; she said those words to Miriam now, "Ha-Makom yinakhem otkha b'tokh sh'ahr avalei Tzion v'Yerushalayim." Beth still remembered what they meant: May the Almighty comfort you among the mourners of Zion and Jerusalem.

Miriam recalled the time of Shivah. Mirrors were covered since the vanity of what a person looked like really did not matter at such a time. The men were unshaven as well—again reminding the mourners that the things of the flesh had little importance during death. People sat on low stools and even on the floor. Every attempt was made to become as meek and humble as possible. Death was an equalizing force among all people and had a very real ability to provide perspective. Beth thought of Easter time when their pastor washed the feet of some of the congregants, just as Christ had done. It was a time for the priest to become as humble as possible and serve just as Jesus did. Humility was the key virtue of a disciple.

Beth could see that it all reflected her own Catholic faith which was filled with sacramentals—those things that one could see and touch and feel and do and thus be more transformed in spirit. People were, after all, very tactile in nature so it made sense that when trying to get to his or her most spiritual self—that place where God resided—a person was aided in his or her efforts through visible, tangible means. During Shivah, even the food was symbolic. The food served was all round in nature which represented the circle of life. The tables were filled with hard-boiled eggs, bagels, and chick peas. A minyan—a group of ten men—was always present and prayers were constantly being offered. The entire experience transcended the earthly and Beth was forever affected by its beauty and piety.

Miriam's words roused Beth from her memories of Shivah in the Goldfarb home. "I have to go home and tell Joseph's parents. I can't let this news come from his superiors or from anyone else. They can't hear the words of the death of their beloved son without knowing of his sacrifice and heroism. I'm afraid anyone else just wouldn't be able to explain all this to them."

Beth heard the sorrow in Miriam's voice and knew that it would be foolish to try to talk Miriam out of accomplishing this task. Even though, from Beth's perspective, Miriam was too wounded for such an undertaking. Memories of Ayala's death flooded Beth's heart in empathy for Miriam. *How much pain and sorrow could one person be expected to experience?*

So, instead of pointing out the obvious, Beth chose to encourage her friend. Surely if Miriam felt she needed to do this, trying to stop her would only put an obstacle between them and may also give Miriam regrets for the rest of her life. Those "would-haves" and "should-haves" often became the emotional downfall of many.

Elizabeth agreed, "Yes, I understand. You two had a very special relationship and it is right for you to make sure his parents—and sisters—knew of his great personal sacrifice for the mission and for whatever else…"

As Beth's words trailed off, Miriam seemed to latch onto the unspoken point to which Beth now made. "I know that these past few days have been ordained by God. They have been filled with His presence and His power. I pray that Joseph's sacrifice has been in accordance with God's will. Joseph was so bent on serving God and I have been so blessed to have known and loved Joseph." Miriam thought of Joseph's proclamation of his love for her—and his desire to know Jesus. She knew her life would never be the same even while she could not explain what that meant at this point in time.

After a few minutes of silence, during which Miriam was clearly playing the past few days over in her mind, Beth questioned her, "When was the last time you ate something?"

Just as she asked, Luke walked out of the bathroom. He was washed up and had changed his shirt. Hearing Beth he offered, "I can make something of the few things we bought yesterday at the market. How about a simple cheese omelet?" At home Luke was pretty famous for his omelets. The kids loved to make crazy requests and watch him turn them into works of art— both visually and epicurially. It actually all started one weekend morning when the kids were young and had just heard Luke read *Green Eggs and Ham* by Dr. Seuss. Luke teased them that they *would* like green eggs and ham and so the breakfast gauntlet had been laid down! It had evolved over the years but was always fun for both Luke and the kids.

Miriam murmured that she couldn't possibly eat but Beth persisted—still very much in mother-mode. "You have to eat something even if it is just a bite or two."

Maybe Miriam could see that you couldn't fight Beth and agreed that a bite or two she could handle. Luke got busy in the little galley kitchen while Beth and Miriam sat in a silence that blanketed each with love and comfort. No words were needed; neither felt compelled to offer any to her friend.

"Ok! It's ready," Luke summoned them from their cocoons and each wordlessly obeyed the call.

Once seated, Luke pulled out a book from the cupboard. He explained to Miriam that the owners of the apartment had stockpiled different drawers and cupboards with books filled with prayers and words to contemplate. He found a prayer in one he felt especially fitting. It was from the Dead Sea Scrolls and Luke read it in a quietly reverent voice.

> *Author of my well-being, Source of knowledge, Fount of holiness, height of glory, All-mightiness of eternal splendor! I shall choose that which He shall have taught me and I shall rejoice in that which He shall have appointed unto me. I shall bless His name; when I go out and when I go in, when I sit down or when I rise up, and upon my bed shall I sing unto Him. I shall bless Him with the offering which comes forth from my lips for the sake of all which He has established unto men, and before I lift up my hands to partake of the delicious fruits of the earth. Amen*

Simultaneously Miriam and Beth said, "Amen."

"I feel terrible that you went through all this trouble," Miriam said to Luke. "I am really not hungry at all."

"It was no trouble." Luke promised her and it was clear that he meant it. They had all been through a difficult and draining time and cooking was Luke's way of getting his mind off things. Miriam intuitively understood about escape and smiled as she picked up her fork and using its side cut off a small piece of the omelet. Delicious smells wafted to her nose and seemed to signal to Miriam's stomach that nourishment would be good for her. She dug in; Luke and Beth followed suit and silence once again was the order of the day.

Within minutes all the omelets had been consumed—including Miriam's who admitted, "Well, I guess I was hungrier than I thought."

Elizabeth smiled and said what she knew to be true in these circumstances, "Your mother would be glad to see you eat."

There were almost too many levels to this statement and Miriam's eyes welled up as the thought of the compote her mom used to serve her when she was a young girl and had experienced a particular incident at school that was disheartening—or in some way just needed a mother's love which always arrived in the form of a meal and a loving word. "Yes," Miriam acknowledged, "Emma would be happy to see me eat."

They got up from the table and walked the few steps to the seating area. The sounds from the streets below had ceased and Miriam wondered out loud what would happen next, "The pope is safely ensconced in his Vatican apartment. The rabbis and cleric have been whisked away from the chaos in the Colesium and Joseph is dead. It is time for me to move on; but to where? To do what?"

Luke didn't feel it was quite his place to be part of this conversation and excused himself to put on a pot of coffee—something he was sure they all could use. As he walked towards the kitchenette area he heard Beth say, "God will guide this and His will is going to prevail."

Chapter Thirty-One

*For I know well the plans I have in mind
for you, says the Lord, plans for your
welfare, not for woe! Plans to give you a
future full of hope. When you call me,
when you go to pray to me, I will listen to
you. When you look for me, you will find
me. Yes, when you seek me with all your
heart, you will find me with you, says the
Lord, and I will change your lot.*

~Jeremiah 29:11-14

Miriam left her time with Beth and Luke holding a book that Beth had given her. One of the many books that had apparently filled the little apartment. Somehow, Beth said, she knew that they weren't meant only for the occupants but were for any given situation. Like God's gifts, they had the most value when given away. So it was that Miriam had in her hand a book on Edith Stein.

Although Miriam couldn't imagine reading anything at the moment, she had to admit that she felt the same about eating and then had proceeded to gobble up the omelet. She trusted Beth and knew her to be a woman who followed the nudging of the Shekinah. Beth referred to this spirit of God as the Holy Spirit—and Miriam was well aware of this moniker since that is how the pope came to be called the White Dove in their mission. The dove being a symbol of the Holy Spirit—what the Christians considered the third person of the "Trinity."

All of this interested Miriam, especially since she knew it had engulfed Joseph in his last days on earth.

He had gone from being a pragmatic Mossad agent to a spiritual, selfless agent of God. He seemed to have grasped the attempt on the life of the White Dove to a much greater degree than the other agents—Miriam included. Joseph seemed to have answers that were more supernatural than natural; and what intrigued Miriam was that Joseph seemed fine with that conclusion.

†

The quick cab ride to the airport didn't allow much time for Miriam to think about anything other than how she would break the news to Joseph's parents. She only needed to make a phone call to her home office to get a flight arranged and by the time she arrived at the airport, everything had been done. She simply printed out her boarding pass at a kiosk and made her way through security. Her identity was known to those who handled her ticket and she was easily able to get on board the commercial liner with no problems. In any other situation, having no luggage would have prevented her from boarding as this would have been quite suspicious—as would have been her one-way ticket; but all this had been cleared and she had no worries, other than the huge concern of meeting Joseph's parents with the news.

Just the thought of Joseph made her heart ache. It was a different ache than she had for her mother. When she thought of her mom the ache was for what had been. Miriam was well aware of what she would no longer have when her mother died. On the other hand, Miriam realized that the ache she had for Joseph was for what "might have been." It sounded too corny—too much like a line from a movie. But it happened to be the truth. She could close her eyes and see Joseph's smile, hear his voice, and feel the warmth of his body next to her. She thought about his coordination of the

Four Horsemen project and her heart skipped a beat. He was a brilliant man. He was kind and he was fun. A life with Joseph would have brought great joy to Miriam. She thought of her parents and how much they had enjoyed the life they had shared together. She thought of the laughter that was often heard in their home and she thought of the ways in which they loved and respected one another. She knew that would have been her life with Joseph.

Do you not want me to be happy in my life? She queried God. Oddly she had no recrimination towards Him, mostly she just wanted to know and asked another question of her Creator: *If not Joseph, then who? Or what? What do you want of my life, Adonai? I am Yours.*

†

Once everyone was on board, it was only a matter of minutes before the plane departed for Israel. Miriam looked at the book in her lap and decided that sleep could wait. The questions she posed to God were now hanging out there like the clothes her mother used to pin to lines across the balcony. They would blow this way and that, depending on the wind; but sooner or later they would be dry. Her questions might also be blown about, but sooner or later she knew she would have an answer.

She just didn't expect it so soon.

Chapter Thirty-Two

*The kingdom of heaven is like a treasure
buried in a field, which a person finds and
hides again, and out of joy goes and sells
all that he has and buys that field.*

~ Matthew 13:44

Miriam awoke when they landed. Her plan had been to read but she could not keep the heaviness from her eyes and they promptly closed as soon as she felt the plane lift off the ground.

Now she was home and ready to tackle the task ahead. She hailed a cab and gave an address and instructions to the driver. She would be at Joseph's parent's home in less than half an hour. She had decided that calling ahead would only set off anxiety since she would not be able to answer what she knew would be their questions about Joseph. *How are you, Miriam? And how is Joseph? Is he with you?*

These were things that she couldn't bear handling over the phone. The sleep she had on the plane was enough for her to feel rested and now she spent the time in the cab praying. She asked for God's wisdom so that her words would offer love, condolences, and maybe one day, peace. She didn't make any plans on what she was going to say, rather, she let God know that she would rely on Him for counsel.

As the cab pulled up to the small but neatly kept residence, Miriam paid the driver and walked to the door. She wasn't sure anyone would be home but also left that to God. His timing was, after all, always perfect.

And if this wasn't the entirely correct time to tell Joseph's parents about his death, she would walk to a neighbor and use a phone to summons another cab to take home.

One quick set of knocks—maybe more timid than they ought to be if they were truly interested in drawing someone's attention to answering the door—were immediately answered. The door opened and Joseph's beautiful mother stood smiling at Miriam. "I heard the cab pull up and peeked through the front window."

So much for my "super-agent" skills, Miriam wryly said to herself. Within a few seconds, Joseph's father was standing in the doorway as well. He stood a bit behind his wife and over her left shoulder. They were both wearing casual clothes and were clearly enjoying a relaxing day. The temperature was warm but not too much so, the usual humidity was absent. Joseph's father put his right hand on his wife's left shoulder and somehow Miriam knew he knew. His hand went from his wife's shoulder to her waist where with one hand on each side he seemed to be prepared to steady her for what he anticipated was coming. He gently guided her to the side and said to Miriam, "Please, Miriam, come in." They had met only once before but, like Meir and David were aware of Miriam's feelings towards Joseph, Benjamin Klein knew that his son was in love with this woman. And now she stood before him with some news to tell.

Maybe sensing something in the hands placed at her waist, Marcy Klein quickly said, "Is everything okay?" even as she was being moved to the side so that Miriam could gain entrance to their front room. Miriam remained speechless as she stepped across the threshold and caught out of the corner of her eye that Marcy's legs began to buckle. Just as Luke had given Miriam the strength one short day ago, so was Benjamin now giving strength to his wife.

"Mr. and Mrs. Klein," Miriam began but was immediately interrupted.

"Please, do call us Ben and Marcy," Joseph's mother requested.

"Thank you. Ben. Marcy. This visit was supposed to be to announce that Joseph and I were to get married." Miriam wasn't sure why those were her first words; but, trusting in the guidance of God she saw their wisdom as tears began to roll down Marcy's face. Although Miriam did not know of Joseph's phone call a couple of nights ago to his mother, those memories were now flooding Marcy's mind and heart.

Miriam continued, "My guess is that you both must have known how Joseph and I felt about each other long before we knew! I know my dad and brother will tell me the same thing." Somehow Miriam managed a quiet laugh that filled the room with the love that had been Miriam's and Joseph's. All three occupants could feel the intimacy they shared in the knowledge that Miriam and Joseph had so deeply, so unwittingly fallen in love. The quiet laughter was perfectly placed—a gift from God—as its sincerity was found in the depths of Miriam's heart.

"Yes, dear Miriam, I believe we've known longer than you two," were the kind words that Ben offered. His large hand was covering Marcy's folded hands upon her lap. Miriam detected that he squeezed them and assumed that both he and his wife had probably discussed this very thing.

"So then you know that I loved him first as a friend and was eager to love him as a husband."

Miriam found she could not swallow—the lump in her throat felt enormous—even painful; she unsuccessfully fought back tears and simply stopped talking. She was forced to sit, like Marcy, with her hands in her lap.

After a few minutes of silence, it was Marcy who stood up and walked over to Miriam. Marcy knelt in front of Miriam and put her hands over Miriam's, very much the same way that Ben had just been covering her own. She compassionately looked Miriam in the eyes and said in the most loving of voices, "Miriam, we, too, were eager for the life that you and Joseph would have shared. We know that he loved you as a friend and also looked forward to loving you as a wife. There was nothing more we could have asked for as his parents."

Marcy knew that she and Ben had been blessed to have had Joseph for many years and their sadness existed in the knowledge of what Miriam would now not experience. They were unshaken in their awareness that Joseph was a man of great virtue. He was a man unlike many other men, willing to put others first. He would have brought great joy to Miriam—and for that Marcy was incredibly heartbroken for the woman who sat before her now.

Ben sat in his chair and gazed out the window. He could see Joseph playing as young child, chasing after his sisters and throwing the ball to friends from the neighborhood. Ben could feel Joseph's hot, sweaty little body against his when he came into the house after those simple childhood days.

Ben recalled when Joseph told both his parents that he was joining Mossad. All the moments of Joseph's life in their home and family washed over Ben like the sea washes over rocks on the shore—and Ben knew that his life had been very blessed, indeed, to have been Joseph's father.

In many ways Ben knew Joseph to be a far better man than he had ever been and silently offered the *Mourner's Prayer* for his dead son.

> *May His great Name grow exalted and sanctified in the world that He created as He willed. May He give reign to His kingship in your lifetimes and in your days, and in the lifetimes of the entire Family of Israel, swiftly and soon.*

> *May His great Name be blessed forever and ever. Blessed, praised, glorified, exalted, extolled, mighty, upraised, and lauded be the Name of the Holy One Blessed is He beyond any blessing and song, praise and consolation that are uttered in the world.*

> *May there be abundant peace from Heaven and life upon us and upon all Israel. He who makes peace in His heights, may He make peace, upon us and upon all Israel. Amen.*

Chapter Thirty-Three

God infuses into man, over and above the
natural faculty of reason, the light of grace
whereby he is internally perfected for the
exercise of virtue, both as regards
knowledge, inasmuch as man's mind is
elevated by this light to the knowledge of
truths surpassing reason, and as regards
action and affection, inasmuch as man's
affective power is raised by this light above
all created things to the love of God, to
hope in Him, and to the performance of
acts that such love imposes.

~ St. Thomas Aquinas

Miriam knew that her father and brother were at the beautiful Moked Rosh Bed and Breakfast on the Sea of Galilee in Northern Israel. "Moked Rosh" literally meant "hidden treasure" and by all accounts that is exactly what it was for her parents: a hidden treasure. Meir and Ayala had made it a yearly trip to celebrate their anniversary and had never gone a year without spending a few days relaxing and enjoying the incredible sights and sounds of the largest freshwater lake in all of Israel—the hidden treasure. The water itself had many names such as the Lake of Galilee, the Lake of Gennesaret, the Sea of Tiberias, and the Waters of Gennesaret; but no matter what name was used, Miriam was always fascinated by what the rabbis said about it: "Although God has created seven seas, yet He has chosen this one as His special delight." When Ayala died, David would not let his father forgo this favored tradition. David began, then, to accompany his father to the B&B and they would fish and pray and relax.

Whenever Miriam thought of the Sea of Galilee, she smiled. It is fed by rain, springs, and the Jordan River which is where she and Sipporah—Joseph's beloved sister who would soon be receiving the news about his death—had "kidnapped" Elizabeth on the last full day of her Holy Land trip. They had taken her to the Jordan River to do a bit of guided white-water rafting. The day had been overflowing with love and laughter and had been the perfect ending to a trip that was filled with a roller-coaster of experiences and emotions—just as their canoes had been overflowing with water!

The Sea of Galilee is about 20 kilometers long and maybe a bit more than 10 kilometers wide which means that from the peak of Mount Arbel on the western side of the lake you can see it in its entirety. Miriam had taken Joseph there on more than one occasion where they would spend time talking about their families and their lives. Joseph was able to—certainly without being aware of it—break into the darkness of Miriam's life. Their conversations were natural and their ability to understand one another was remarkable. No doubt being able to take in the incredible sight that lay before them added to the moment; they talked and gazed at the city of Tiberias, the mountains of Galilee, and the Golan Heights. Now, as Miriam thought about the Gennesaret Plains below the cliffs of Arbel—which ran along the northwest shore and were known far and wide (even from the times of Josephus) for their incredible beauty and ability to nurture any plant—she knew that if heaven existed upon earth, this spot must certainly be it. She recalled how the great historian wrote about the moderate temperatures and the varied species of flora that grew to create the characteristic beauty of the Plains and that she had given Joseph a book about it. Joseph loved to research things and Miriam loved history—all this just one more way they seemed destined to be together.

She remembered a particular time they were at the Sea of Galilee and the way in which a storm quickly whipped up the peaceful sea. It was most alarming to watch until Joseph shared with her some of his mother's favorite Bible verses. He talked about Jesus being able to calm storms and of walking on water. Joseph was clearly intrigued by the idea of it all and as the sun set that day, he was lost deep in thought about this man Jesus. Miriam shared some of her own knowledge and even now, simply recalling the conversation, Miriam felt as if God's hand had been upon them and guided their talk. *Could they have imagined that just a few short months later Joseph would have given his life for others? Could they have even imagined how they would stand on the Coliseum grounds and listen as a rabbi spoke of Jesus being a "fisher of men" and calling everyone to the same task?*

Here, Joseph and Miriam had sat and talked as if their entire lives were ahead and that their words were nothing more than a fascinating conversation in which they could share their interests and ideas. She remembered how she felt that day. Her heart was filled with a new depth of love that she had never felt for anyone else. It was different than the love she had for her family. She hadn't recognized it then, but she knew now: it was agape love. Joseph had spoke of it before. It was the love of the Creator. It was the love of the Savior. It was what was behind Jesus giving His life for sinners.

Miriam's breath caught in her throat and a bead of sweat made its way down the back of her neck.

She could hear him talking of love to her that day and with a quickening in her heart knew that he hadn't just been sharing the idea of love—he was professing his love to her. She also realized that it was a love that would grow exponentially from that day on Mt. Arbel because Joseph had opened his heart to it, in some way, at the impetus of the Four Horsemen mission. He then offered it to his fellow man in the most selfless of acts a person can perform—to give his life.

> *If I speak in tongues of men and of angels, but have not love, I am a noisy gong or a clanging cymbal. And if I have prophetic powers, and understand all mysteries and all knowledge, and if I have all faith, so as to remove mountains, but have not love, I am nothing. If I give away all that I have, and if I deliver my body to be burned, but have not love, I gain nothing.*

†

Miriam opened the door to the empty apartment. Her father and brother would be home the next day. Her dear friend Elizabeth—and Elizabeth's husband, Luke—were on their way home to America. While Miriam had been there, their daughter Sophia had called and expressed great concern as the television stations and Internet were filled with stories of murder and mayhem taking place in Rome. News of the attempt on the pope's life and then the death at the Coliseum were unnerving Sophia. Luke used all his business connections to get them an earlier flight home. They all knew it was the right thing to do.

Miriam also knew that God had taken care of her to have placed them—Beth and Luke—where they had been at that precise moment in time so that they could tend to Miriam when she was in desperate need. Miriam could feel her mother's presence as well. Everything she had learned about God and faith and trust were coming into play in her life. She was no longer a Mossad agent and knew it. She wasn't quite sure what she was—but she could feel that God was calling her to something different.

She was tempted to turn her computer on and see what the latest news in Rome was but thought better of it. She had a full day and a half before her father and brother would return home and she determined that the best way to spend that time was in quiet and in prayer. She had the book Beth had given her and felt she needed to read it. Miriam had often found solace in books and this time would be no different. After the death of her mother, God invited Miriam deep into her faith. Her appetite for books became ravenous. That is when she came across the works of Josephus, the renowned historian, and other more recent works. She read through the *Megillah* and spent more time learning about her namesake: the sister of Moses. Now, as at that time, she could feel her body ache as it yearned to be filled with the sort of knowledge that was found in books about the events and people of the past. She could feel a desire well up within her to know how she was connected to the past but also had a place in the future. Just as her body required food and water, so, too, did her soul require the wisdom and knowledge of God found in the lives of the Tzadikim—the righteous ones. To her these necessities were all inseparable if she were to live.

Her soul now needed to hear words of life and love and Miriam expected to find them in this precious book her friend had given her on Edith Stein—a fascinating woman who gave her life—completely, freely, and ultimately literally—to God. She was a Catholic saint—to Miriam a tzaddik. Miriam knew tzaddiks to be those virtuous men and women who were now in the presence of God. Jewish laws were clear that one was not allowed to call upon the dead; but asking for the intercession of the righteous ones was not, according to many Jewish books such as the Talmud and many Jewish teachings such as Jewish mysticism, in violation of that abomination. As the rabbis explained, it is an ancient custom to visit the gravesite of the righteous and plead for their intercession.

The most well-known of these instances, and one which all Jews were expected to look to for understanding, was the case of Caleb. Moses sent out twelve spies to the land of Canaan. Miriam reflected on the twelve stone statues of the apostles that lined St. Peter's Square and understood that number. The twelve spies that Moses selected represented the twelve tribes of Israel; surely this was also why Jesus chose twelve apostles.

What Moses wanted of the twelve spies were answers to such questions as to the quality of the land and the people who inhabited it. Of the twelve spies, only Caleb and Joshua were said to have brought back positive news. According to Jewish teaching, this was because Caleb had first visited the burial places of the great Jewish tzaddiks Abraham, Isaac, Jacob, Sarah, Rebecca, and Leah. Caleb implored their intercession and he was given a very different understanding of the land of Canaan!

Further study of the difference between the abhorrent practices of beseeching the dead versus imploring intercession of another, whether living of dead, explained that when one Jew asks another for intercession, the person asked shares in the need of the request. Since all were seen as one body, this sharing of one another's joys and pains and sorrows and needs put a request for intercession in a very different light than calling upon the dead. It was a matter of enjoining one another—whether on this side of eternity or the other—rather than being seen as individual needs. When one person in the Jewish body was in need, all were in need. Thus Caleb was able to stand at the graves of his righteous ancestors and ask for their help—and receive it.

As Miriam continued to read she could easily see that Edith Stein—St. Teresa Benedicta of the Cross as she became known—was one such woman: a saint and a tzaddik.

Miriam was absolutely transported into another world as she read the book on this incredible woman. Miriam was one of those readers who used a marker to highlight the "important" parts: passages and points that she would go back to and revisit. Words that she would contemplate and bring into her consciousness in a real and meaningful way.

Not long into reading the book on Edith Stein, Miriam realized that the entire book thus far was highlighted! There was nothing in the book that did not fascinate and inspire its reader. God surely guided Elizabeth when she gave the book to Miriam. With each new sentence, and each new revelation about Stein, Miriam could feel the hole inside of her own body closing, mending, become whole again. "Hole, whole, holy," Miriam said out loud as she recalled Beth talking about her spiritual director guiding her from hole to whole to holy. Miriam could feel that happening to her now—she felt herself moving from hole to whole and knew that God would continue to lead her through the journey to holy.

The pages of the book were speaking to her more than any other work had in her life. She did not need to meander through them for them to become real; their reality was palpable the moment she read them and their meaning reverberated in her spirit like the chords echoing from Sipporah's harp. In the past few days— and certainly in her lifetime, Miriam could see that God had provided the foundation upon which He was now building. Drawing her home; allowing her to seek His treasures.

Miriam recalled how the melody Sipporah would often play seeped into her soul and felt that these words were doing the very same thing, but plumbing her depths even more—which Miriam wouldn't have imagined possible. The nights in which their friends would gather and listen to Sipporah's masterful rendition of whatever newest piece she happened to be inclined to play for them were some of the most mystical experiences Miriam had ever had as a young adult. Now, reading about Stein, Miriam was again reminded how something could transcend the natural and live in the supernatural.

Edith Stein wasn't just a woman whose life was being revealed within the pages, she was Miriam's spiritual sister. Miriam's connection to her transcended the natural—it truly felt supernatural. It was spiritual in essence even while Miriam would be hard pressed to describe it; Edith and Miriam shared a rich and vibrant heritage and, somehow, also Miriam's future. Miriam instinctively knew that the answers she sought were in the pages that lay open before her.

†

Stein was an intellectual giant. Miriam couldn't find any other way to describe the woman whose life was so quickly and profoundly affecting her own. Born on Yom Kippur in the year 1891 was a foreshadowing of the life that was to unfold for Edith. Yom Kippur, being the highest of holy days for the Jewish people, is the day that each asks God to be written in the Book of Life. No doubt Edith's birth on this day must surely have been written on her mother's heart in a very special way.

Elizabeth once talked about the things that Jesus' mother had kept in her heart. That image—that a mother may hold a secret, mystical knowledge about her child—seemed very appropriate to now attribute to

Edith's mother. The youngest of eleven children, this future Carmelite nun was known to be a very sensitive child. Both physically and emotionally, Edith bore the consequences of living as a perceptive soul. It could not be a surprise that she would later be known as a mystic given her particular awareness of people and events. Her father died when she was just a toddler, surely making her sensitivities all the more prevalent.

Due to her immense intellect, this young German Jewish girl decided, in her early teens, that God did not exist. Stein considered herself a "thinker" and couldn't fathom how a "God" could fit in. Ironically, the more Stein learned, the more she saw that God was the only answer!

It wasn't a coincidence that Miriam had also gone through that same experience in her teens. Although she certainly didn't consider herself an intellectual equal to Stein, Miriam could recall her almost insatiable need to learn about any and everything when she was young. In that way, her connection to Edith seemed solid. It also was a foundation from which God could easily call a person. After all, the more one learned about God, the more one could come to see His truths and the reality of His existence.

So it was that Edith took that same course: standing firmly in reason, she decided God did not exist. From there, God allowed her to meander here and there and connect with other intellectual giants of her time where conversations could tackle the depths of life and truth. It is probably best to say that when Edith was ready, God provided an opportunity for her to see His face.

That opportunity came in two distinct ways. A friend died and Edith was able to see firsthand that the widow was a devout woman who found comfort in her faith. The year was 1917.

The other profound experience that Edith had was when she picked up a copy of the autobiography of St Teresa of Avila. The year was 1921 and in a now-famous remark, Edith is known to have said when she finished the book: "This is the truth."

Indeed, thought Miriam, *this is the truth!*

Edith Stein was baptized into the church on January 1, 1922. Miriam thought about her own parents and how they would react to her choosing to leave the Jewish faith. However, the more Miriam read the more she felt it wouldn't really be leaving—just as Edith must have surely known—it would be more like "completing" a journey. Of course, Miriam's father would not see it that way—nor would her mother have seen it that way. So when Miriam read that upon hearing of her daughter's conversion, Frau Stein cried—as did Edith, Miriam totally understood. *One would have been tears of sadness and the other tears of, what? Tears of sadness to have hurt someone you love and yet tears of joy?* Miriam moved around uncomfortably in her seat at the idea of it all. *And yet who could deny God when He called?*

Although Edith immediately wished to join a convent, she was advised against it by her spiritual director. Since Elizabeth often spoke of her own spiritual director, Miriam was getting quite comfortable with the idea of that sort of authority in the life of someone desiring to grow closer to God. Edith's spiritual director seemed to want her to wait, pray, and discern further about entering a convent since initial passions after baptism often run high and wide. He wisely may have thought that once a bit of time went by Edith's interest in the convent would wane. But it never did.

So, in obedience, Edith spent many years teaching and allowing God to use her to His ends until the time came when she could join the convent. In retrospect you could see how God used each piece of Edith's life—that she freely offered to Him—so that she could be molded and conform herself completely to God.

All the while she was reading, Miriam kept thinking about the remarkableness of this woman who made it all seem rather easy—not difficult and not messy. No one could deny that it was anything but easy and clean; and yet Edith Stein—St. Teresa Benedicta of the Cross— once yielded to God, made it all seem rather simple indeed.

During the time that she waited out her ability to enter the convent, Edith wrote numerous essays and was very influential in the lives of the countless people who attended her lectures or read her works. In fact, people were still reading them—just as Miriam was doing now. She admitted that she found herself completely absorbed in the words of this mystic who was killed in 1942 at Auschwitz.

This is the truth! Miriam admitted once again as she sat in the quiet of the room. This is the truth Joseph surely discovered.

Now what?

†

Miriam looked at the clock and realized that she had read and re-read the book for more than seven hours. And those seven hours felt more like seconds—if that. Miriam felt as if she needed to learn more while at the same time understanding that she knew enough. She closed her eyes and God took her to a place of love and comfort. He took her into His arms and proclaimed His great and unending affection for her. She was His beloved.

†

Miriam awoke to the sound of her father's voice and the gentle cajoling of her brother's hand upon her shoulder. She had been in a very deep sleep; one from which she did not wish to arise. She was safe with God. The idea of separating from Him was too much to bear and she let her brother continue his efforts to pull her from her sleep. *If only he knew,* she said to herself in her slumber, *he would let me be! He would let me stay in this place of happiness and peace!*

"Miriam, sheyne meydel," Meir said to his sleeping daughter. Meir purposely chose to use the Yiddish term for "beautiful girl" just as Ayala often had when she called out to Miriam.

Deep in her conscious, despite her efforts to stay asleep, Miriam roused upon hearing her father call her "sheyne meydel." Her eyes fluttered open and David lifted his hand from her shoulder. Both were bent forward and had concerned smiles of their faces; neither having ever seen Miriam asleep in the living room.

Once her eyes were fully opened, David walked towards the kitchen to put on a pot of coffee. He pulled out compote from the fridge and heard his father pull up a chair next to Miriam. Meir remained silent, as did David. Each waiting for Miriam to direct how the conversation would go. If something were wrong, Miriam would choose the time and place to share it; both father and brother had learned that Miriam's need for privacy, coupled with the nature of her often-secret work, was more a test of their patience than anything else—simply because their concern for her was always their first priority.

Miriam smiled at Meir and offered her thanks to David when he brought the hot cup of coffee, "Toda."

David, too, pulled up a chair so that Miriam was now flanked by father and brother. If she was unable or unwilling to share what had caused her to fall asleep in the living room, she at least knew that her family would surround her with love—literally and figuratively.

"I hope you both had a wonderful time," was how she chose to begin.

"It was wonderful, indeed," Meir responded. "Everything was perfect, from the weather to the food to the fishing. I believe Adonai allows this to be so for my benefit."

This was the first David heard his father say such a thing and asked, "Why Abba?"

"Well, since this was such a special place for your mother and me, God isn't allowing it to be anything less than perfect each time I am there. He knows that I have already suffered enough with her death and I think He just wants to make sure I'm okay!"

David smiled and said, "You are right, Abba. God is that good." To himself David realized that God was beyond good: his father had clearly not seen the skies filled with clouds, felt the sprinkles of rain each day, or recognize the lack of fish as compared to previous years. Yes, God was good.

The three sat in silence for a bit more, each sipping coffee and taking bites of compote. David had pulled back the curtains and the sun filtered through the windows. It was going to be a beautiful day. After a while, Meir decided it was time to share with Miriam that Joseph had contacted him and had sent a package.

"Joseph called me about a week ago. We had a wonderful conversation. He is a mensch, Miriam."

At the mention of his name, along with her father calling Joseph a mensch—a truly good and righteous man—Miriam's eyes filled with tears. "Yes, Abba, Joseph is a mensch."

Her father continued. David already knew the gist of the conversation as he had also had one with Joseph— at Joseph's request. David was impressed with this young man and knew that Miriam would be very happy in her life with him. "We talked quite a while. I know that he wants to spend his life with you and I have given him my blessings."

At that, Meir stood up and walked over to the end table where, on the lower shelf, sat a small box. He picked up the box and brought it back to Miriam. Placing it on her lap, he said, "Joseph asked me to give this to you when I saw you. I don't know what is inside but can guess!" Meir had no idea that with each word he spoke Miriam felt as if a sword were being plunged into her heart.

Looking down at the box on her lap, Miriam wasn't sure if she could open it. Her hands felt weak, feeble. *How could the same hands that held Joseph as he died now open a box that was from him and meant for their future?*

"I would have imagined you tearing it open!" David teased.

Miriam looked from her father to her brother and back to the box. With shaking hands and trembling fingers she opened the small box. There was no ribbon and no wrapping paper. Simply an unadorned box. Inside of it was a velvet ring box and a card. She opened the card first. In it, Joseph had written out the psalm of love.

I am my beloved's and my beloved is mine. If you will say yes, I will spend the rest of my days showing you my love. Your beloved, Joseph

Miriam then opened the ring box which held her intended wedding ring upon which was inscribed the verse in Hebrew that read *Ani L'Dodi V'Dodi Li*. The last words Miriam spoke to Joseph: "I am my beloved's and my beloved is mine."

לי ודודי לדודי אני

Miriam's tears fell upon the ring and she looked up at her father. "Abba, Joseph has died. He has been killed."

Meir could not believe the searing pain that ran through his stomach upon hearing those words. This could not be happening. It seemed impossible— unfathomable—that God would allow this to happen to Miriam! Meir was overcome with grief and confusion. It was almost too much to bear.

Looking at Miriam, Meir knew that if there was anything he could have done at that moment to replace his daughter's own pain with joy, he would have done it. Nothing had ever felt more pressing to him than to be able change this moment from sadness to the elation. And in his inability to do so, Meir felt like a complete failure as a father. If a parent cannot protect his child from the worst sort of pain and sadness that can be experienced, then what was the use? Although he didn't know it, Meir was crying. All the years of holding back his tears came flooding out in one vulnerable moment. And once they started, Meir had no way to stop them or get them under control. He wanted to rage at Adonai while also flee to Him for comfort. The contradiction of his feelings was too much. His heart was in a tailspin.

David took his father's wrinkled, aged hands and looked him in the eye and prophetically said, "Abba, a father's job is to provide love and comfort and shelter—and you've done that beyond measure. Both Miriam and I know that if you could remove this pain from her heart, you would in an instant. You would not even hesitate…"

Then David turned to Miriam and held her hands and said, "For that I know Miriam is grateful." Miriam nodded in agreement as David spoke. As he continued, David's words brought comfort and hope.

Beyond sadness, past pain, lived the truth of a father's love. And in that truth, Miriam would live and hope and one day rejoice.

Miriam lived in she'mamah for quite a while. In this wilderness—she'mamah—she continued to study and seek God. She often wrote to her dear friend Elizabeth and kept her apprised of the ways in which God was leading Miriam. Beth always wrote back and her words were encouraging but also smart, intelligent. Beth wasn't one to get carried away and make rash decisions. She had learned a lot in her life and had found a way to iron out the roller coaster emotions that had plagued her in her young adulthood and early in her marriage.

This made her the ideal confidante for Miriam. Miriam also sought her own spiritual director and ultimately made life-changing decisions along the way. She was able to leave Mossad and had also been able to take a trip to America where, for a few days, Elizabeth and Miriam connected in a deeper way than ever before. Somehow they must have known that it would be their only time together and each could feel a melancholy as the days wound to a close. But they each trusted God and knew His plans for their lives would be far richer than anything they could imagine. The time they spent together created a bond, a basis, upon which God would move each woman forward in new and loving ways. Miriam saw it as that "cornerstone" that others had rejected and knew that Joseph had helped lay the first building block for her life in Christ in the conversations they had shared while in Rome.

†

Three years after Joseph's death, Miriam wrote one last letter to Beth.

Dearest Beth,

How can I ever begin to explain to you what your friendship has come to mean to me? Words are inadequate as I look back and see how God's hand has been upon us the whole time. How could one ever explain it all? From the moment you first imagined taking a trip to the Holy Land I believe that Adonai, blessed be His Holy Name, also began making plans for our friendship! How can it be explained otherwise? It cannot, as I'm sure you will readily admit.

Think about this Beth, you were there when the two most important people in my life died. When my mother was killed, you tended to me with the same motherly love that she had always given me. When Joseph died, you were there as well. If we don't believe in God we still could not deny the immense consequence of all this; but since we do believe, then we owe Him gratitude for His unending care for us. But even in the midst of those words, how can one ever explain the Father's love that has given us His Son? Our mere human experiences as parents or children or friends or spouses are only a glimpse of the love that awaits us in Heaven if we only freely accept it now.

So much has happened in these past few years. Your country has gone through political and social changes that have, I am sad to say, cast it upon a road that leads away from God. How long will He wait for its complete contrition and return? What I have come to understand is that people such as yourself who continue to believe and fast and pray have successfully stayed the Hand of Judgment. But for how long? I wonder what people need to see before they will fully and firmly believe. I pray for them.

Rome was a taste of repentance and redemption in our lifetime. Was the earthquake the day of the vote for unlimited, tax-funded abortion a coincidence? Again, as a believer we can't call things coincidences—it dishonors God who continues to pull back the veil between heaven and earth and invite us in.

If the final days of evil come in our lifetime, Beth, I know we will be able to fight the good fight because of what we have gained from our friendship as sisters through the blood of Christ—through God's grace. Joseph already fought the good fight. Joseph could see how we each are being asked to give of ourselves. He was an incredible man; as my father has said, Joseph was a mensch. He died in my arms and I know that he was surrounded by angels who ushered him to the heavens even as tears rolled down my face. Dare I believe that his act of selflessness stayed the hand of God? I do dare to boldly believe such a thing. I believe that the Four Horsemen mission and the words spoken in the Coliseum made a difference, too.

These aren't just the ramblings of a broken or desolate woman. As we have already shared with one another, we saw the angels, we know of God's presence that day. God has given us these glimpses so that we can prepare. Prepare for what? I'm still not sure. It is clear that we have more questions than answers; but if we had all the answers, what role would faith play in our lives? And trust? All we've been given is a unique piece of the puzzle. As the rabbi said that day, we have been individually summoned. Are we responding? Are we each doing our part? We've seen the church elect a new pope; a man of courage and conviction. He will not be loved by all; he will have a difficult time. But he is a man of Christ, a humble servant. The rabbis who were being protected and the Muslim cleric were all men of great honor. They were all willing to offer the ultimate sacrifice:

their lives. They all spoke truth. This is what is important: truth.

There were more envelopes to open and read from on that day in the Coliseum. Where they are now, I do not know. Again, more questions than answers; and yet there is peace for those of us who are walking in freedom—the freedom that comes from Christ. I live in amazement every day, Beth. Jews call this sort of amazement "pli'ah." It is the ability to look around and see God. It is how Joseph lived the last days of his life. Despite what was happening, he was able to make a decision to offer this life. He chose to believe in the goodness of man and mankind and to offer his life for many. He became in that one act a complete disciple. Many of us aren't able to do this—nor are we asked to do it; but Joseph was both: he was able and he was asked. He allowed God to use him as an instrument of love and sacrifice; and I am forever grateful to have known Joseph.

Remember that book you gave me about Edith Stein? Again, God's hand. Here was a Jewish woman who also recognized truth. She saw it in Christ—just as Joseph did—and has helped me see it in Him as well. Joseph set the foundation and God used the words and life of Edith Stein to build upon that foundation. I joined Mossad after my mother was killed so that I could have an active role in the destruction of terrorism and in the building up of a nation of peace. I find it providential that while that remains constant in my heart's desires, the way I will now help accomplish it has changed. Edith Stein spent many years from her entrance into the Catholic Church until she was able to join the Carmelites. During that time she spoke to countless people and wrote life-changing essays. While her heart yearned for the Carmelite order, she followed the suggestion of her spiritual director and waited to make that commitment. What she gave to the world during that time continues to live on today—showing the wisdom of her spiritual director, to be sure! I feel such a parallel in our lives—hers and mine. I feel as if my destiny was waiting for me but that I had a journey to take that would best prepare me for it; and now the time has arrived for me to step into it. I see all the building blocks that God used along the way—just as he did for Edith.

I entered the church this past Easter. My father and brother were in attendance. While they are certainly having difficulty, they have done their best to support me. Then, on August 9th, I entered a cloistered community. The Carmelites, to be exact. Just as St. Teresa Benedicta of the Cross did when she was Edith Stein. When Edith entered the Carmelites it is written that all those whose paths had crossed with hers—students, colleagues, people who attended her lectures—became part of her daily prayers. Can you see God's awesome hand in that? That is how I feel now: everyone who has ever been part of my life is now part of my prayers! What an honor and a privilege God has given us to pray for others. That is how God is now inviting me to be part of the peace He desires for us: I will now spend my days in prayer and contemplation of His goodness and mercy. I understand all the pieces of my journey thus far and am humbled by God's great love.

I wanted to share with you some of the words of Edith Stein that greatly affected me. Here, as only someone who has experienced the Jewish faith can truly do, she writes of the Holy of Holies. I wept at reading her words and the truth they revealed. Let me share them with you, here:

"The individual human soul a temple of God—this opens to us an entirely new broad vista. The prayer life of Jesus was to be the key to understanding the prayer of the church. We saw that Christ took part in the public and prescribed worship services of his people, i.e. in what one usually calls "liturgy." He brought the liturgy into the most intimate relationship with his sacrificial offering and so for the first time gave it its full and true meaning—that of thankful homage of creation to its Creator. This is precisely how he transformed the liturgy of the Old Covenant into that of the New.

"But Jesus did not merely participate in public and prescribed worship services. Perhaps even more often the Gospels tell of solitary prayer in the still of the night, on open mountain tops, in the wilderness for from people. Jesus' public ministry was preceded by forty days and forty nights of prayer. Before he chose and commissioned his twelve apostles, he withdrew into the isolation of the mountains. By this hour on the Mount of Olives, he prepared himself for his road to Golgotha. A few short words tell us what he implored of his Father during this most difficult hour of his life, words that are given to us as guiding stars for our own hours on the Mount of Olives. "Father, if you are willing, take this cup away from me. Nevertheless, let your will be done, not mind." Like lightning, these words for an instant illuminate for us the innermost spiritual life of Jesus, the unfathomable mystery of his God-man existence and his dialogue with the Father. Surely this dialogue was life-long and uninterrupted. Christ prayed interiorly not only when he had withdrawn from the crowd, but also when he was among people. And once he allowed us to look extensively and deeply at this secret dialogue. It was not long before the hour of the Mount of Olives; in fact, it was immediately before they set out to go there at the end of the Last Supper, which we recognize as the actual hour of the birth of the church. "Having loved his own…, he loved them to the end." He knew that this was their last time together, and he wanted to give them as much as he in any way could. He had to restrain himself from saying more. But he surely knew that they could not bear any more, in fact, that they could not even grasp this little bit. The Spirit of Truth had to come first to open their eyes for it. And after he had said and done everything that he could say and do, he lifted his eyes to heaven and spoke to the Father in their presence. We call these words Jesus' great high priestly prayer, for this talking alone with God also had its antecedent in the Old Covenant. Once a year on the greatest and most hold day of the year, on the Day of Atonement, the high priest stepped into the Holy of Holies before the face of the Lord "to pray for himself and his household and the whole congregation of Israel." He sprinkled the throne of grace with the blood of a young bull and a goat, which he previously had to slaughter, and in this way absolved himself and his house "of the impurities of the sons of Israel and of their transgressions and of all their sins." No person was to be in the ten when the high priest stepped into God's presence in this awesomely sacred place, this place where no one but he entered and he himself only at this house. And even now he had to burn incense "so that the cloud of smoke…would veil the judgment throng…and he not die." This solitary dialogue took place in deepest mystery.

"The Day of Atonement is the Old Testament antecedent of Good Friday. The ram that is slaughtered for the sins of the people represents the spotless Lamb of God. And the high priest descended from Aaron foreshadows the eternal high priest. Jesus Christ anticipated his sacrificial death during the last supper, so he also anticipated the high priestly prayer. He did not have to bring for himself an offering for sin because he was without sin. He did not have to await the hour prescribed by the law, nor to seek out the Holy of Holies in the temple. He stands, always and everywhere, before the face of God; his own soul is the Holy of Holies. All who belong to him may hear how, in the Holy of Holies of his heart, he speaks to his Father; they are to experience what is going on and are to learn to speak to the Father in their own hearts."

St. Teresa Benedicta's words continue to live and grow inside of me and her example of love for God is, now, the truest, most pure fulfillment of the words Joseph and I shared with each other. They are words which I now intimately whisper to Hashem: Ani L'Dodi V'Dodi Li.

Regardless of the distance between us, my heart is always with you, sweet sister in Christ, and I look forward to the time when you and I meet in Heaven where there will be no more tears and we will stand face to face with Christ and enjoy the Father's glory.

Sister Edith Elizabeth

CPSIA information can be obtained at www.ICGtesting.com
Printed in the USA
BVOW07s0642140813

328348BV00001B/3/P